Madhav Sharma

OTHER INDIAINK TITLES :

FORTHCOMING TITLES :

Madhav&Kama

A Love Story from Ancient India
Translated from the Sanskrit

A.N.D Haksar

IndiaInk
ROLI BOOKS

Lotus Collection

© A.N.D. Haksar, 2006

First published in 2006
The Lotus Collection
An imprint of
Roli Books Pvt. Ltd.
M-75, G.K. II Market, New Delhi 110 048
Phones: ++91 (011) 2921 2271, 2921 2782
2921 0886, Fax: ++91 (011) 2921 7185
E-mail: roli@vsnl.com; Website: rolibooks.com
Also at
Varanasi, Agra, Jaipur

Cover image : courtesy Roli Collection
Cover   : Arati Subramanyam
Layout : Narendra Shahi

ISBN: 81-86939-24-5

Typeset in Baskerville by Roli Books Pvt. Ltd. and
Printed at Anubha Printers, Noida

P.M.S.

In Remembrance

Vaman Shirodkar

E.P. Bharata Pisharodi

M.S. Padmanabha Sharma

my Sanskrit teachers at different times

Contents

Introduction

❧

$\mathcal{J}$he tale of Madhav and Kama, or Mádhavánala and Kámakandalá to give the protagonists their full names, is an ancient Indian love story. It was probably in oral circulation well before the written form. The Sanskrit text, presented here in translation, is notable for its simple yet evocative language, its dramatic setting of scenes and its candid portrayal of both the physical and the emotional aspects of attraction between people in love. It was current till about a century ago, but then seems to have faded, becoming virtually unknown to modern readers.

The story's oldest recorded manuscript is dated Samvat 542 which, if taken to be the Nepali era, would correspond to AD 1422 though its language may suggest a somewhat earlier date. Titled Mádhavánala Kathá, it was located in the Durbar Library of Nepal. A scholarly study[1] lists forty three other Sanskrit manuscripts of this tale. Dating from the sixteenth to the nineteenth centuries, they lie at places as far apart as Thanjavur and Varanasi, Pune and Kolkata, Gujarat and Kashmir, besides copies which have found their way to collections in Britain, Italy and Russia.

The titles differ. A common variation is Mádhavánala Kámakandalá Kathá. In some texts the word kathá is substituted by ákhyánam, upákhyánam or kathánaka, which also mean a tale, or by kávya, a poetic composition. In some others, interestingly, the word used is nátaka or nátaka kathá, which indicates that the narrative was also used as a play. But the storyline, style and literary structure are broadly the same in all cases, pointing to an underlying unity in what may be different recensions of the same material.

From the number, geographic distribution and differing dates of these manuscripts, it would appear that the story was current over a large area for a long period of time. This is also borne out by its retellings in other Indian languages, specially in the north and the west of the country. Texts of these versions exist in old Gujarati, Rajasthani, Marathi, Hindi and Urdu, the last being a translation from Braj Bhasha by Mazhar Ali Willa under the title Quissa-i-Madhunal.

One version occurs in the Sikh Guru Gobind Singh's Dasam Granth[2] which, together with another verse retelling in Sanskrit dedicated to the Mughal emperor Akbar, formed the basis of the long narrative poem Mádhavánala in seventeenth century Hindi by the Muslim poet Alam. From such data it would seem that the original's appeal had also transcended sectarian and cultural divides. Such plurality in its currency is not surprising, given the universal nature of the story's theme – the joys and sorrows of true love, and the vicissitudes of two young lovers amidst their romantic meeting, sad separation and final reunion.

~

The Madhav-Kama story forms part of the kathá literature of classical Sanskrit. This comprises a variety of narratives, sometimes in verse, but more often in prose interspersed with gnomic and descriptive stanzas. The famous Sanskritist Winternitz[3] divided them into four groups: popular tales of oral origin; fables and stories intended for inculcating worldly wisdom; others compiled for religious propagation; and those meant essentially for entertainment. These were composed in relatively direct and easy to understand language, in contrast to the more cultivated and ornate kávya style of a fifth group of narratives which include celebrated works like Dasha Kumára Charitam of Dandin and Bána's Kádambari[4]. The kávyas were written mainly for cultured and sophisticated audiences. The simpler kathás, on the other hand, catered to a wider cross-section of society. The tale presented here has elements of all the four groups outlined by Winternitz; but though it includes sage precepts and pious passages, it is primarily a romance, meant more to entertain rather than edify its readers.

This story is also a part of the considerable Sanskrit literature about the exploits of Vikramaditya, the famous king and hero of Indian folklore. The best-known and already translated works from this group are Vetála Panchavimshatiká or Twenty-five Tales of the Vampire and Simhásana Dvátrimshiká or Thirty-two Tales of the Throne.[5] Others include Shálivâhana Kathâ and Vira Charitra, which are about Vikramaditya and his successors; Vikramodaya, in which he appears in the guise of a wise parrot; and Panchadanda Chhatra Prabandha, in which he is a mighty magician.[6] In the romance of Madhav and Kama, the king features as the third principal character, through whose extraordinary efforts the two lovers are eventually reunited.

~

Not much can be said about the author of this work. Of the forty four existing manuscripts, only fourteen cite one by name. In three it is given respectively as Vidyápati, Kavishvara and Kanakasundara. The first two of these, it has been surmised, could also be honorifics. The remaining eleven manuscripts name the author as Ananda or Ananda Dhara, and five of these further describe him as the pupil of Bhatta Vidyá Dhara[7]. Modern scholarship has, as such, generally ascribed the work to Ananda, a disciple of Bhatta Vidyá Dhara[8].

Unfortunately, in common with many other Sanskrit authors of antiquity, nothing is known beyond the name in this case. One historian[9] of Sanskrit literature noted at least ten writers called Ananda, and speculated that the author of this work might be the same as a commentator styled Ananda Rájánaka. This title, referring to a government functionary, was used in Kashmir where the title Bhatta, or the learned, was also prevalent. The detail could have helped to place the author geographically if the identification was conclusive. At present, however, apart from the author's name, we have only the story attributed to him. The story in brief follows:

Mádhavánala is a well-born, musically talented and very handsome young man in the city of Pushpávati. People complain that he is turning the heads of all the women in the town, who are getting infatuated by his beauty. The king summons him to the court for a musical test, and banishes him on discovering that the queen herself and her ladies are no less affected by his charms.

The young man finds his way to the city of Kámávati where the lovely dancing girl Kámakandalá happens to be performing before Kama Sena, the ruler. He impresses the latter with his knowledge of music and dance, and is honoured with a special gift. But the ruler feels affronted when Mádhavánala publicly presents that gift to the dancing girl for her virtuosity, and she in turn praises him lavishly for his judgement and generosity. The king then angrily orders the youth to leave his kingdom.

On his way out of the royal court, Mádhavánala meets Kámakandalá who, too, has been smitten by him. She takes him to her house where the two engage in banter, fall in love and spend the night together. They play literary games, cap verses, solve riddles, and impress each other with their skills. They are distraught when

Mádhavánala is obliged to leave the next morning amidst emotional farewells.

Both are lovelorn in their separation and exchange long messages as Mádhavánala wanders from place to place. Eventually, he arrives in Ujjayini and takes shelter in the temple of Shiva, Mahákála, there. Pining all the while for Kámakandalá, Mádhavánala expresses his anguish in some verses he writes on the wall of the temple.

The writings stir the curiosity of King Vikramaditya of Ujjayini, who is famous as the Dispeller of Others' Sorrows. A courtesam helps him locate Mádhavánala and the king questions him about his problem. Unable to persuade him to forget and give up Kámakandalá, the king realizes that the young man is truly in love, and decides to unite him with his beloved. To this end he proceeds with Mádhavánala to the city of Kámávati.

In order to test Kámakandalá's love for Mádhavánala, King Vikramaditya first meets her secretly. He propositions her and, on being spurned, tells her that the man she loves is dead. The dancing girl collapses and dies on getting this news. When her death is reported to Mádhavánala, he too follows suit. Stricken with remorse, the king is set on suicide, but his familiar spirit, the vetála saves the day by fetching the nectar of immortality with which the two lovers are brought back to life.

Thereafter, Vikramaditya negotiates with King Kama Sena of Kámávati through an emissary for the release of Kámakandalá, and finally forces it after a battle. He then reunites the two lovers who return with him and live happily ever after.

~

The story also sheds light on contemporary social conditions. Some are well known, for example, feudal kingship and caste hierarchies. The existence of highly cultured and economically independent courtesans is also found in other works: Kámakandalá has been compared to the high-minded Vasantasená in the classic Sanskrit play Mrchhakatika. A feature of the present tale is its description of a music concert and a dance performance. It also describes samasyá vinoda, a literary pastime deserving some mention.

Samasyá Vinoda consisted of setting propositions or riddles for explanation or solution by the other party, often in improvised verses. The prahelíká or riddle was a recognized part of literature: sixteen varieties have been listed in Kávyádarsha, a well-known seventh century work on poetics by Dandin[10]. The hero and the heroine give several examples of these in their exchanges during their first meeting.

Of the locations mentioned in this tale, Ujjayini is readily identifiable with the present city of Ujjain in Madhya Pradesh. Still held in tradition as the old capital of Vikramaditya, it is also the site of the famous Mahákála temple, last rebuilt in the eighteenth century. Kámávati is harder to locate in the absence of any evidence. But some data which may be relevant to Pushpávati is deserving of notice here.

This is a reference in the old Central Provinces Gazetteer of the then Jubblepore district, pertaining to a place known as Bilahri in Murwara Tehsil near Katni in modern Madhya Pradesh. It notes that, according to tradition, Bilahri was a flourishing city in the distant past, and was then known as Pushpávati. It was found by the colonial recordist to contain many old structures and remnants, among them a ruined temple known as the palace of Kámakandalá. 'Local tradition,' he wrote, 'avers that Mádhavánala, the hero of the well-known drama, was resident of Bilahri. He was a great vocalist, but he displeased the king and was banished. He thereupon went to the court of Kama Sena, who had a dancing girl named Kámakandalá. They married and returned to Bilahri with the assistance of another king and constructed the building which goes after his wife's name.'[11]

It may be inferred from the note cited here that the locale of our story lay probably in an area of modern Madhya Pradesh, where it was still known in tradition when the gazetteer reference was compiled in colonial times. According to separate reference, from the Archaeological Survey of India report for 1924-25, Bilahri may have been the capital of the Kalachuri kings in twelfth century AD. The historical basis, if any, of the tale of Mádhavánala and Kámakandalá is obviously a subject for further academic research, as indeed is the gamut of its various literary aspects.

Available records show that this research has received comparatively little attention so far. The Sanskrit text of the tale has been published only on two occasions. The first was in Italy nearly one hundred years ago.[12] The second was in India three decades later, but merely as an appendix to the text of a popular Gujarati retelling, and without any translation or further comment. The sources were described in some detail in another study of a later Sanskrit retelling[13], but the text of the original has remained largely unexamined. Standard histories of Sanskrit literature, when they mention the tale of Mádhavánala and Kámakandalá, do so very briefly. As far as it was possible to ascertain, it has never been translated into English.

~

The present translation is intended to bring this once popular and still charming love story before the English reading public of today. The text I have used is entitled Mádhvánalákhyánam and reproduced, as mentioned above, in the appendix to the Gujarati Mádhavánala-Kámakandalá-Prabandha, edited by M.R. Majumdar and published in Baroda in 1942 as the Gaekwar Oriental Series No. 93 .[14] Majumdar ascribes it to Ananda, though the appended text itself does not name any author.

This Sanskrit text, which I have translated completely, is written in Champu styles, which mixes prose with verse. Mainly in the former, it is interspersed with 233 verses, of which sixty nine are in Prakrit or Apabhramsha. Some are quotations from other classics while others may be originals composed for the story. Most have been rendered in prose to maintain cohesion and continuity in the translation of the narrative. Nearly half, however, have been presented, where it seemed suitable, in free verse form for closer correspondence with the original and to convey some of its flavour. In such cases they have been marked serially, and the original stanza numbers from the Baroda (or Ananda) text have been listed in the endnotes to facilitate further reference.

The translation has been supplemented with extracts from some retellings which provide further details of the story absent in the Baroda text. Three retellings have been utilized for this purpose: one in Sanskrit and the other two in old Rajasthani. The material taken from them has been identified in the endnotes. Whether it is derived from some contemporary oral tradition, or is the reteller's own embellishment, remains an open question.

The Sanskrit retelling is titled Mádhavánala-Kámakandalá-Carita. Ascribed to Jodh Kavi, a court poet of Akbar, it has a dedicatory shloka to the emperor and another dating it, unusually, to a year in the Hijri era corresponding to AD 1583. It was edited in 1953 with a learned introduction and annotations by Dr Balbir Singh who has pointed out that its text is distinct from the Baroda text in that it is entirely in verse and has significant omissions and additions. The extracts I have incorporated in the present translation appear as the second prefatory verse, some descriptions of the hero and the heroine and their dialogues with Vikramaditya, and the account of the royal envoy Shripati who is not mentioned in the Baroda text at all.

The two vernacular retellings are taken from the appendix of the Majumdar edition already mentioned. Both are in verse. The first is Mádhavánala Kámakandalá Chaupai by Váchaka Kushala Lábha. Completed in Jaisalmer in AD 1623, it consists of 662 verses, including forty one in Sanskrit. The other is Mádhavánala Kathá by Kavi Damodara, written in Vadanagar, AD 1681. This contains 793 verses, including thirty in Sanskrit.

Several Sanskrit verses in both Lábha and Damodara are identical with those in the Baroda while others are new additions, some of which I have used to supplement the translation. The account of Kama's previous incarnation in paradise is taken largely from Lábha, as also the poignant shloka with which the king informs Kama that her lover is dead. The Afterstory is also taken from Lábha and placed as an appendix to separate it from the account in the Baroda text of which it appears to be a later continuation. The episode of Madhav's encounter with Queen Rudra, some details of his talk with Vikramaditya and some of Kama's dance are derived from Damodara.

The hero's name is often abbreviated to Madhav and the heroine's occasionally to Kama in all the texts cited here; this usage is also reflected in my translation. Jodh Kavi further uses the short names Nala and Kandala in a few places; but only the latter has been used here.

~

In translating from the Sanskrit, both of the Baroda text as well as of the retellings, I have endeavoured to combine fidelity to the original with the requirements of modern English usage; the rendition of vernacular extracts has generally been through paraphrase or a further retelling. The division of the whole into chapters with separate titles has been done for ease of reading, and does not reflect the original, which is a continuous text with its own invocatory and closing stanzas, here placed, respectively, in a prologue and an epilogue. Textual, mythological and other references have been given in the endnotes which also include explanatory information on items such as the sixteen ornamentations and the sixty four arts. Spellings follow the standard pattern, except that some names still current have been spelt as is usual at present. Diacritics are confined mainly to long vowels.

~

Research for the present work has strengthened an impression I had formed earlier in the course of similar studies: that there is a wealth of material in the treasure trove of Sanskrit kathá literature still waiting to see the light of day through appropriate translation. Some little-known tales have already been mentioned in this note. References to many more are buried in literary histories or their footnotes, or in the numerous catalogues of manuscripts at academic institutions.

In present popular perception, Sanskrit is best known as the language of religion and philosophy. The overwhelming majority of readily available translations from its literature are of scriptural and related works, with others like those of didactic fables, erotic treatises and classic plays and poetry following far behind in numbers. The kathá works are even less represented in translation. If more were available to modern readership, it would help to give greater exposure to the secular face of Sanskrit and to its often neglected role as literature whose reach went beyond sacerdotal and societal elites to more popular audiences.

~

I learnt about the text of this tale originally from Dr Anthony K. Warder, Professor Emeritus of Sanskrit, University of Toronto, who suggested it, along with some others, for possible translation from Sanskrit. My first grateful acknowledgement is, therefore, due to him while placing this work before readers. The next is to Dr Narendra K. Wagle of the same university in Canada, who kindly procured a xerox copy of the text for me from the Robarts Library. Subsequently I was able to consult the retellings appended with the text through the libraries of the India International Centre and the Sahitya Akademi in New Delhi. My appreciation is due to Chief Librarian H.K. Kaul and his associates Sushma Zutshi and K.N. Jaha at the India International Centre, and to Librarian M. Vijayalakshmi and her assistant S. Padmanabhan at the Sahitya Akademi, the latter two also enabling me to see the publication containing the Jodh Kavi text. I further thank Ambassador Deb Mukharji for information about the Nepali era and Dr Prem Swarup Gupta for explanation of an obscure verse in the Baroda text.

I would also like to thank Renuka Chatterjee for her ready response, which encouraged me to proceed with this translation. Recognition is due to Nandita Bhardwaj for editing the typescript. Work on this book began at the home of my daughter Sharada, and ended of the home of my son Vikram and daughter-in-law Annika. My love and warm thanks to all three. Lastly, but most of all, I am deeply grateful to my wife Priti for being a pillar of support in more ways than I can ever enumerate fully in this as in all my undertakings.

Manila   A.N.D.H.
24 March 2005

Prologue

With all devotion
I salute Sarasvati[1],
whose vehicle is the swan,
and, by her grace,
narrate this story. (1)

May that goddess,
radiant as
the autumn moon,
dispel all darkness
from my mind
and illumine
my words with meaning. (2)

The Ladies of Pushpávati

༄

here was once a city named Pushpávati, the finest in the whole wide world. Its inhabitants were healthy and long-lived, and so contented and free of fear that it seemed as if time stood still for them. The king of this city was Govinda Chandra. He had seven hundred queens, the chief of whom was the noble lady Rudra.

Queen Rudra had all the signs which denote good fortune. She was in the full bloom of youth. Her eyes were large and beautiful, and her lips red as the bimba fruit[2]. Dark black tresses surrounded the full moon of her face and heightened the classic curve of her bosom. Her movements were graceful and gentle. Altogether a delight, she was sweet of speech and also very clever, bold and proud. She was a shyámá, a term which indicates a woman who has not yet borne a child, or one who speaks pleasantly and may have a dusky complexion, or simply a girl in her sixteenth year.

Women are of four types[3]. The first of these is padmini, or the lotus-woman. Her attributes are: eyes like blooming lilies, small nostrils, breasts set close together, long hair and slender limbs. She is decorous, soft-spoken, and fond of music and dance. Slim and well dressed, her body wafts the scent of a lotus flower. It is said:

> Full-moon face, enormous eyes,
> rounded breasts and tender limbs,
> fragrant like a blooming lotus,
> a shyámá, fair and prolific,
> shy withal, but skilled in pleasure,
> swanlike in her voice and gait,
> respectful of the gods and elders:
> that is the woman padmini. (3)

The second type is chitrini, or the picture-woman, and these are the signs of one: she is dark and slender, with a face like the lotus and the eyes of a fawn. Her voice is like the peacock's and her gait slow and dignified. She has a slim waist and high breasts. Artistic and skilled in musical lore, she is affectionate, loves children and enjoys talking to others. She is just like a picture, say the great poets in proclaiming her chitrini.

The third is shankhini, or the shell-woman. She is slender, with a largely hairless skin. Of a haughty mien, she tends to flit from place to place like a bee, has a wicked sidelong glance and a throaty, purring voice. She prefers wearing red garments and keeps her hair long. But she is not refined and enjoys roughness in making love, such as scratching with the nails. She is also indiscreet by nature.

The fourth is hastini, or the elephant-woman. She is described as short and plump, with a thick neck and large breasts. Her lips are red, complexion fair and her hair sparse and blonde. She moves slowly and exudes a scent like that of the elephant's ichor. She is very fond of good food and quite brazen with men. It is only with much effort that she can be brought to a climax during intercourse.

These types are also categorized as maid, young woman, matron and crone. A girl is called a maid at sixteen years of age and a young woman at thirty. After crossing the fiftieth year she becomes a matron and, after the sixtieth, a crone, deprecated by people as devoid of all worthwhile characteristics.

Mádhavánala

The king Govinda Chandra was a connoisseur of all types of women. In his capital there was also a man-about-town called Mádhavánala, a young brahmin with the good looks of the god of love, the intellect of the celestial sage Shukra and the learning of the divine preceptor Brihaspati.[4]

It is said that Mádhavánala was adept in playing the lute. Every morning, after a bath, he would take the instrument in his left hand and strum upon it softly as he would go to pray at Shiva's temple. On his way home he would also chant verses from the different scriptures.

His was a joyous voice, with notes as sweet as the koel's and as deep as the rumbling of a cloud. The mantras he sang to the accompaniment of the lute charmed birds in swarms and moved even inert objects.

They also attracted the hearts of women, including the proud ones.

Some women followed this lute-player like elephants in musth; some were so entranced that they fell to the ground like does struck by the love-god's arrows; others, gone to draw water, were moved exceedingly and had no peace thereafter.

Though preoccupied with household duties, these women could not forget the man. The sound of the lute made them feel weak. Some laughed insanely and some wept again and again. Some turned ascetic, their bodies besmeared with ashes.[5]

It was not only the brahmin's lute which disturbed the peace of Pushpávati. His handsomeness too had so enchanted all the city's womenfolk that they were driven mad with desire for him. As it is said:

> On seeing a handsome man,
> smelling fresh and clean as can,
> women's pubes
> will turn moist,
> like an unbaked pot
> with water in it. (4)

The Test in the Assembly

❦

*O*nce the citizens came to King Govinda Chandra and addressed him with due respect: 'Your Majesty, your subjects are being ruined by Madhav. The women forget their household duties and wander here and there. Unless he is sent away, all of us will be obliged to leave Pushpávati and go somewhere else.'

'One should not disregard the voice of the majority,' the king said to himself, 'irrespective of whether it consists of good or even bad people. Ants can consume even an elephant when it is weak and trembling.' Pondering thus, he summoned Madhav to the royal assembly.

'O you Madhav,' he ordered when the brahmin had presented himself, 'demonstrate your talents before me, here and now.'

'Why is the king interrogating me like this today?'

wondered Mádhavánala. 'Perhaps some villain of a slanderer has worked on him.

> 'The villain has a dozen mouths
> for speaking ill of others;
> for searching out another's faults
> he has a thousand eyes;
> and of hands no less a number
> for robbing good men of their money. (5)

> 'A villain spies another's fault
> no bigger than a mustard seed;
> his own, of a wood-apple's size,
> he sees but disregards. (6)

> 'There is no house, no royal court,
> not even a prayer hall,
> where you will not find some villains,
> angry for no cause at all. (7)

'What is more,

> 'Though censured, good people
> say nothing improper,
> the cane though crushed,
> gives only of sweetness;
> as for the base, though
> adorned with great merit,
> even in jest they speak
> words which cause conflict. (8)
> 'Villains are like pots of clay,

easy to break, hard to join;
the good are as a golden jar,
hard to rupture, simply sealed.   (9)

'Keep grinding sandalwood,
it still stays fragrant;
keep chopping sugar cane,
it still stays sweet;
keep heating gold,
it still retains its shine;
the good remain the same
even at death's door.   (10)

'As the juice of the sugar cane
gets sweeter with each morsel,
so is friendship with good men:
with villains it is the reverse.   (11)

'The potter's pot, the villain's thought,
once knocked down, will never mend;
but cups of gold and noble hearts
can be put right in the end.   (12)

'Snake and villain, both are wicked,
the last more cruel than the first:
a snake will yield to charm and potion,
who can quench the villain's thirst?   (13)

'Advice offered to a fool
riles him, it never pacifies:

> like milk given to a serpent
> just its venom multiplies. (14)

'But, good or bad, I have to carry out the king's command,' Madhav said to himself. And picking up his lute he struck the notes of a raga, the high, the low and the sublime. In a voice as sweet as nectar he then sang the six ragas and the thirty six raginis in their various modes, octaves and scales. He combined soft tones with sharp pluckings of the lute. His beautiful music pierced the hearts of the seven hundred queens and enchanted the entire assembly.

The ragas he played were: Shri, Vasanta, Panchama, Bhairava, Megha and the sixth, Natta Náráyana.[6] It is said:

> All hail to Music
> the fifth of the Vedas,
> a joy for the happy,
> a solace for the sad,
> its sound steals the heart,
> it's the vanguard of Kama
> loved by all women,
> and easy to learn
> for those who are clever. (15)

Who will not cultivate music? It bewitches animals, not to speak of men. It delights even the gods, what to say of poor kings. It spreads salvation – then, why seek material gain? It is indeed dear to the whole world. The mere thought of it enables the wise to transcend this difficult worldly round. The great god Shiva is himself immersed in the ocean of music.

Madhav's singing left the king wonderstruck. He then put the young man to another test. Having spread sesamum seeds on the floor, he had some women seated on top. The king was amazed when he found the seeds sticking to the backs of their skirts; all of them had experienced orgasm by looking at Madhav.

It is said that, to the great indignation and anger of the king, Queen Rudra herself climaxed at that time. According to another version, she had met Madhav on an earlier occasion and declared her love for him. 'You are the life of my life,' she had pleaded, 'take pity on me.' 'But you belong to someone else,' he had remonstrated, 'love with me can only cause trouble.'

However the queen had persisted. 'I love you truly,' she had said, 'I will protect you. No one will know.' But the youth had been firm. 'Listen, mother,' he had replied, 'your lord is like my father. The sun rises only in the east. How can one even talk about that happening in the west?'

'Beware, Madhav!' the queen had then threatened. 'I have loved you all my life, and if you spurn me I will destroy you. You will be exiled.' He was unmoved. 'Whatever is fated will happen,' he had said. 'I do not care for death or wealth, mother. But if I do what you say, it will be a sin. It is better to die than to live with remorse.' Queen Rudra was furious and later told the king that the city had become impossible because of Madhav.[7]

Whatever the reality, the king thought deeply, even as he marvelled greatly. It has been said:

> Too great a beauty ruined Sita,
> Ravana perished for too much pride,
> Bali fell by extreme charity:
> excess of every kind avoid.[8]   (16)

Having deliberated on all this, the king gave Madhav the threefold betel leaf of ritual dismissal. 'O brahmin,' he said, 'I command that you should no longer stay here.'
    It is said:

> If the father sells the son,
> if the mother gives him poison,
> if the king robs all one has,
> what's the point of lamentation?   (17)

> For the brahmin, humiliation,
> for the wife, a separate bed,
> for kings, defiance of their order,
> is like killing them, it's said.   (18)

Bearing all this in mind, Madhav left the country for foreign lands. Roaming around the world, as the poets say, enables one to see a variety of activities, to appreciate what distinguishes good people from bad and also to understand oneself.

Kámakandalá

◦◦◦

_P_assing from forest to forest and from village to village, Madhav at last came to the city of Kámávati. Its king was Kama Sena, a high-minded ruler. A scholar and well versed in politics, he was adept in dharma and a benefactor of the aged, his thoughts always dwelling on righteousness in every thing. All the four castes were under his influence and followed him implicitly.[9]

In the city there lived the courtesan Kámakandalá, who was in beauty like Rati[10], the love-god's consort. She had enormous eyes and a face as well favoured as the moon. Her ears were like the love-god's noose, her arched eyebrows like his bow and her cheek as radiant as the moonbeam. Her nose was as a pretty tila[11] blossom, her teeth as bright as pearls and her lips the colour of coral. The conch shell's curve adorned her throat and her hair had the splendour of a peacock's plumage. Her bosom, redolent of the scent of saffron, shone like the two auspicious peaks of Meru[12]. Her waist was small, no more than a fist, and her deep navel was of a loveliness none can describe. Her legs were long and smooth like plantain stems and her arms like lotus stalks. Jingling anklets reflected the glow of her toenails. Such was the delightful Kámakandalá.

The First Meeting

◆◆◆◆

Once Kámakandalá was dancing before the king. She wore a bodice perfumed with the essence of sandalwood. At that time Mádhavánala happened to arrive at the royal gate.

On hearing the sound of the mridanga drum Madhav addressed the gatekeeper. 'O keeper of the gate,' he declared, 'all the people in this assembly are fools.'

The gatekeeper reported this to the king. 'Some brahmin has just arrived,' he said. 'Your Majesty, he says that all the people assembled here are fools.'

The king was astonished. 'Go and ask that brahmin,' he told the gatekeeper, 'in what way is this an assembly of fools?' The man questioned Madhav, as commanded. 'O brahmin, in what way are the people in this assembly foolish?'

'Among the twelve musicians there,' Madhav then replied, 'the one who plays the mridanga in front lacks a thumb. So the drum's sound misses a beat. And when the beat falters, what dance can there be? That is why they are all fools.'

The gatekeeper conveyed to the king exactly what the brahmin had said and the monarch well understood its purport. 'Fetch that man quickly,' he ordered the minion, who then brought the youth in. The people stared at him, wide eyed. Was he a god, a divine incarnation or a demi-god? They could no more take their eyes off him than a thirsty deer can off water.[13]

The king bowed to Madhav who offered a benediction:

> 'May he whose deeds
> are truly unfathomable,
> who bestrode the world
> even as a dwarf,
> and bridged the ocean
> with rocks borne by apes,
> and raised the mountain
> in the palm of his hand
> for the sake of the cattle:
> may that god protect you.'[14] (19)

Having blessed the king, he stayed silent. The monarch, on his part, was satisfied. He presented to Madhav the fivefold offering of a necklace strung with gems, a golden crown and ring and two earrings of immense value.[15] Showing him all respect, he then invited the young man to sit by his side on the same seat.

It is said that a householder pleases the gods and earns immeasurable merit if he honours a brahmin devotedly, even when he sees one from afar. The gods are of course propitiated in other ways also. Thus the fire deities are pleased by the welcome ceremony, the god of creation by obeisance, the great god Shiva by rising in his honour, Indra and the other guardians by the ritual of suitable seating and the spirits of ancestors by the washing of feet. Ravi, the sun god, is delighted with the gift of incense, the goddess Ramá by an offering of the betel leaf and her divine husband by that of gold. The king was aware of all this. But he reverenced the visitor, not just because Mádhavánala was a brahmin, but also because he was obviously a person of great merit.

It is merit which is honoured everywhere. Lineage by itself is meaningless. People bow to Krishna, not to Vasudeva, his father. Those who recognize merit take delight in it. The bee comes from the forest for the lotus in the lake, not for the frog even though it lives in the same place.

> Worth derives from merit,
> not from a high position:
> does a crow become an eagle
> by sitting atop a mansion? (20)

> Worth is such for those with merit,
> and a fault for those without it:
> river waters may tasteful be,
> but turn undrinkable in the sea. (21)

Though very far the good may stay,
their merit draws one all the way:
the screw pine's fragrance draws the bee
on its own towards the tree. (22)

From merit comes true excellence,
not from pomp or opulence.
We revere not the moon's full orb,
but its stainless crescent garb. (23)

But the wise do not praise their own merit. To do that is like a beautiful woman cupping her own breasts. This gives neither pleasure nor fortune, both of which come only from another person's admiration.[16]

Kámakandalá was wonderstruck. 'This man is adept in all the arts,' she said to herself. 'He knows the rules of Bharata[17] through and through. Today all my art and skill will be fulfilled.

'It is said:

'Whatever one delights in,
to him is like nectar:
a lily to the bumblebee,
to the termite a dried-up tree.
But the bee which kisses
the queen of the forest
knows good taste from bad;
all the poor old termite knew
was to have wood to chew. (24)

'All that I have danced before the king so far has been in vain. Three things are never appreciated: music by a person with no taste; reading which ignores the introduction; and lovemaking with one who does not want it. They are like an ornament without a dress, a meal without any ghee, a song without a tune or copulation without any feeling. What is the point of a song by one who has no voice? It is the same as beauty without virtue, lineage without character or wealth without charity.'

It is said that a person unmoved by a well-sung song or the charms of a young woman is either a yogi or an animal.

> One who does not know the pleasure
> of good music and of literature
> is a veritable beast –
> lacking tail and horns at least –
> if midst men he goes about
> he still lacks feeling, there's no doubt.   (25)

> A mouth without the taste of music,
> nor skilled in elegant words of Sanskrit,
> which has not drunk of lover's kiss,
> is no more than an orifice.   (26)

> The sages say those hands are useless
> which a maiden's breast have not caressed;
> the ear to which the clever message
> of a go-between has never come
> is just a hole; the teeth but stone

which nibble not in love a lip.
What can one do
with a person who
will not love a woman
as much as he can? (27)

Thereafter, when Mádhavánala was seated at the king's
side, Kámakandalá rearranged her costume once again to
allure the assembly. The earlier audience had been
ignorant, she realized, but now she was before an expert.
So she made marvellous use of musical notes in her
prelude and so harmonized their modulation and rhythm
that it melted the very stones of the stage. And all the
while she sang thus before the assemblage she continued,
on some pretext or the other, to caste glances at the young
brahmin[18].

Finally Kámakandalá commenced a very special
dance, displaying all her skills. Placing a bowl full of
water on her head, she clapped on it with her hands as
well as her foot. She juggled tiny balls in her hands and
hid pearls in her mouth. Then, as a large black bee came
from somewhere and was about to sting her on her breast,
she shook it off with a deep breath and the movement
known as the cow's shiver, in which her bosom trembled
without missing any beat of the rhythm or note of
the music.

The superb manoeuvre was noticed by Mádhavánala,
who also observed that the king and the others had
understood nothing of it. 'This is wonderful,' he said
to himself, as he surveyed their vacant faces, 'she shook

off the bee without the king even being aware.'[19] And then he presented forthwith the fivefold offering given to him by the king to Kámakandalá as a due reward.

Kámakandalá received the gifts in both her hands and raised them to her head. 'O Mádhavánala!' she cried, 'you are a repository of the fourteen skills. You are an adept of the seventy-two arts! This is a most noble gift. As goes the verse:

> 'An earring cannot grace the ear
> as does from scriptures' hearing;
> the hand is graced by charity,
> not by bracelets' wearing;
> and kind folk shine by doing good,
> not by using sandalwood. (28)

'But,

> 'This earth is full of many gems,
> and it is not right to wonder at
> man's penance, courage, charity,
> his knowledge and humility, (29)

'For,

> 'If one does not use this body
> to be of help to others,
> then isn't it false flattery
> to trust in it so merrily?' (30)

'The wise give away wealth and even life for another's sake,' she added. 'Their end is inevitable and it is better to renounce them in a noble cause. To live for others is indeed praiseworthy. Even animals live just to fill their own bellies. There is nothing strange in good people always ready to help others. They are like sandalwood trees which do not grow only to shade themselves. Such people, dedicated to the welfare of others and unmindful of their own comfort, are born to benefit the world. Their bounty is the same for everyone, like rain from the cloud, or light from the sun and the moon. Their compassion extends even to the unworthy: it is like the moon which does not withhold its beams from the outcaste's dwelling. Just as rivers do not drink of the water they carry, nor trees eat of the tasty fruit they bear, or clouds shower rain for their own benefit, the greatness of good people is entirely for others.

> 'The good are like great trees
> which fruit to feed others,
> themselves endure the sun,
> and give shade to one and all.'　　　　　(31)

The Banishment

~~~

*T*he king was overcome with jealousy as he observed the gifting by Mádhavánala and Kámakandalá's response. Dismissing the assembly, he turned on Madhav with loaded words. 'O Madhav,' he said, 'why did you give to Kámakandalá the fivefold offering I had presented to you?'

'Because of her glorious performance,' replied Mádhavánala. 'Even animals appreciate the merits of music, though they live in forests. They too have no money, so they offer their very lives to the hunter. The deer's gift to the singing trapper is its life. Blessed is that beast. It surpasses even Bali and Karna in its magnanimity.'[20]

'There is nothing which cannot be perceived through music,' the brahmin continued, 'it is the soul of the world. Without it there would be no Brahma, no Hari, no

Shambhu. With it, the celestial singers brought Madálasá from the dead. No sacred river can lead one to the paradise of Kailasa as does Sarasvati, the goddess of song.'[21]

The king's face darkened. 'You mendicant!' he retorted. 'I would have you beheaded with the sword, except that, as a brahmin, you should not be killed. It is said that those who kill brahmins, cows and specially women go to the worst of hells for millions of aeons. Also that it is impermissible to slay children, people from one's own clan, those whose salt one has eaten and those who come seeking asylum. Therefore, I order you not to remain here any longer. Get out!'

'As Your Majesty commands,' said Madhav, even as he pondered,

> 'Who has ever heard or seen
> in envoys truth, in crows hygiene,
> in eunuchs courage, in drunks thought,
> in snakes forgiveness, even a jot,
> in women passion at an end,
> and a king who is a friend?'　　　　(32)

'I am indeed unfortunate, alas, to be sent away from a place like this,' he said to himself. 'But this is just bad luck:

> 'The sun may rise in the west,
> mountains move, fire turn cool
> the lotus bloom upon a rock,
> what is fated will not change.　　　　(33)

'Is it the tree's fault if the hunchback cannot reach its sweet fruit above, even though its branches bend down under their weight? But one should not blame oneself, nor for that matter another, whether friend or master. The blame lies with the karma of each. For who can wipe off what fate has inscribed on his forehead? It is no fault of the season of spring that kareer trees have no leaves, nor of the sun that owls cannot see in daylight, or of the cloud that raindrops do not fall directly into the chátaka[22] bird's beak.

'Like the shadow which goes with one's own body,' he thought further, 'there is no way in which things can be other than as they will be. One should know that even the assistance of one's mind and thought, and the accomplishments of one's intellect, are as they are destined to be. If there was an antedote to the inevitable, the likes of Nala, Rama and Yudhisthira[23] would not have suffered as they did.'

Hurt no end by the king's insulting behaviour, Madhav walked away. A man insulted will abandon even his parents and relatives, wife and home, land and wealth. He will do so from afar, as if they are poison. As go the verses:

> Shattered is good people's merit
> if indiscriminate the ruler be,
> like the matron's pride and spirit
> when her husband loses virility.   (34)

> You may read with every flourish
> poems to an utter fool,

– 25 –

the wretch won't know it even when
your voice itself has lost its cool:
it's like the woman, moved by love,
who, eager for one last embrace,
leaps into her husband's pyre
but the corpse knows not her face.   (35)

The fool who serves
with hope of gain,
goes many miles
to gain but hope.   (36)

For,

What to say of men with talent,
where talent has no honour true,
in a land of naked sadhus,
what will any laundress do?   (37)

Madhav and Kama

Madhav left the royal palace, reflecting again and again on such thoughts. As he walked out on the road, he was approached by Kámakandalá who was afire with love. 'O my dear, lotus-eyed love-god,' she said with all respect in a most engaging and pleasing manner, 'do me the favour of coming to my home.' And taking him by the hand, she led him to her house.

It is said that at first Madhav demurred. 'Listen, Kama,' he told her, 'I have never had anything to do with courtesans. Why should I come to your house? It will give me a bad name.' But she fell at his feet in tears and his heart succumbed. At her home she entertained him in many ways.[24] It was there, when they were sitting together on a couch, that they fell in love with each other.

Love does not happen
just like that,
but when it does
it's like the shawl
of natural red:
wash it repeatedly –
the colour stays fast.   (38)

A good woman's love
will never falter,
even in another life.
Parted from Krishna,
the Yamuna's waters
are dark like him
to this very day.   (39)

The love of Kama and Madhav did indeed begin in
another life. It is said that she was then a nymph called
Jayanti at the heavenly court of Indra, the king of the gods.
So proud was she of her beauty that Indra cursed her to
become a rock in Pushpávati. She would stay in that form,
he told her, until someone married the rock.

Madhav was the son of Shankara Dasa, a priest in
Pushpávati. The father had been childless and had prayed
for progeny to the great god Shiva, who blessed him with
this handsome and accomplished boy. While still a lad, in
the course of a game with his friends, Madhav had been
married with the prescribed rituals and due ceremony to
the rock which was the nymph.

Released from the curse, the nymph returned to

heaven, but then came back for the boy, with whom she had fallen in love. She told him she was his wedded wife and carried him away to Indra's paradise.

It is said that in heaven the boy Madhav became deeply attached to the nymph Jayanti. He would pine for her whenever she went out, wait constantly for her return and on each occasion when she came back, question her no end. 'Be patient, my love,' she would say, 'I truly love you, but cannot stay here all the time, for I have already been cursed by Indra once before.' Still he would feel restless in her absence and keep looking for her here and there.

However, Madhav enjoyed himself with the nymph when they were together in Indra's land. Once, it is said, she was commanded to take part in a dance performance before the celestial assembly. Not wishing to leave the boy behind, she turned him into a bumblebee and hid him between her breasts inside her bodice, where she could always feel his presence.

The performance commenced, the orchestra played and Jayanti danced her part together with thirty two other young nymphs. But her mind was on her darling and she was brimming with love for him so she could neither keep time nor move her limbs in synchrony. 'Why is this nymph faltering so much?' wondered Indra as well as the other gods and, on examination, they discovered the boy hidden in the guise of a bee.

Indra grasped the situation at once. 'A man has entered heaven by stealth,' he cried angrily, 'and this worthless creature, not content with heavenly company, has been carrying on with him! This is a grave misdemeanour.' Jayanti was sent home and the priest's son was promptly expelled from paradise.

On the following day the distraught nymph was presented before the divine assembly. Indra flared up like fire when ghee is sprinkled over it. 'You enjoy the pleasures of the gods,' he roared, 'yet you are not satisfied, and want in heaven itself the delights which come with a man! Then go to the land of the mortals!' And, because of her unprecedented sin, he cursed her to be born from a harlot's womb and suffer the consequences thereof.

That is how, it is said, the nymph Jayanti came to be born to the courtesan Kama in the city of Kámávati. As pretty as a picture, she was given the name Kámakandalá. At the age of eight she was put to the practice of music, dance and the other skills. She mastered the canon of Pingala[25] and could soon sing like the celestial choristers. By the time she became a courtesan herself, she was proficient in all the sixty-four arts[26] and knew everything about dance and drama. She was by then in the bloom of youth and as beautiful as the celebrated Rambha. All the people who saw her were enchanted by her beauty and skill.

Sitting besides King Kama Sena, Madhav remembered the nymph as he watched Kámakandalá dancing. She had the same champak flower complexion and coral lips, the same serpentine hair braid and undulant gait. Her eyes, like those of a tremulous fawn, her firm, uplifted breasts, slender waist and long legs were the same, as was the radiance of her face, the sweetness of her voice and the way she put a delicate finger to the bright teeth in her betel-painted mouth.

Madhav was overcome as he looked at her and, when the bee hovered on her bosom, his mind went back in time. 'She turned me into a bee in heaven,' he said to himself, 'and hid me between her breasts. Where is that nymph who loved me?' And then it dawned on him that Kámakandalá was that nymph in her previous life.[27]

Love in Union

~~~

*K*ámakandalá and Mádhavánala were sitting together on the couch in her house. 'Such smoothness, my dear!' she said to him. 'To have got inside my heart at the very first sighting! This has to be learnt from experts, but you have done it without even a lesson from anyone.'

'A single hair can stick in the throat and trouble the body,' Mádhavánala replied. 'But you have entered my heart with your entire braid and put it under siege!'

As they conversed with each other, both were overcome by passion. Then commenced a communion of love, wonderful in its limitless variety. What can be said of making love with a damsel both dextrous and devoted? The lustre of the lamp reveals all kinds of happenings, but cannot display where the oil has gone, even though the wick is immersed in it. And the

pleasure which a mature woman experiences in
renewed intercourse creates a sense of beatitude which
the heart knows and remembers, but the tongue can never
express.

> Some are courageous
> in taming mad elephants,
> yet others are skilled
> in slaying fierce lions,
> but rare are they
> who can withstand
> the wildness of love. (40)

Later Kámakandalá gazed at Madhav. 'O my lord,' she
said, 'tell me some riddle or conundrum, or else the night
will pass for nothing.'

Madhav listened, and then asked:

> 'The beauty spot of finest musk
> on your cheek has not been smudged,
> nor the kohl which rings your eyes
> or sandal paste upon your breasts,
> the scarlet on your lips, enhanced
> by juice of betel, still remains:
> tell me, friend, of elegant gait,
> is your lover sleeping, or
> is he just a callow boy?' (41)

Kámakandalá listened to the riddle, and responded in
kind:

'My lover's not asleep, O friend,
nor angry, aged, or a fool;
listen, neither is he false,
leprous, sick, or even dead:
he saw me young and beautiful,
and was by passion so affected
that suddenly his seed got spilt,
confusing the poor dear.'   (42)

They continued thus to amuse each other with banter, wit
and repartee. It is well known that the wise pass the time
in recreation with music and laughter, while the foolish
expend it in quarrelling, vice and sleep.

Realizing that Kámakandalá was extremely
knowledgeable, Mádhavánala posed another question:

'In her chamber at midnight,
the maiden, with a wooden pen,
draws the likeness of a serpent:
say, my friend, for what is it?'   (43)

Kámakandalá replied,

'The maiden is burning
in the fire of separation:
her lover is gone abroad.
On the wall she draws a snake,
and imagines it's a lamp
to illumine the night

from moment to moment,
for it is Shiva's creature
and she is filled with longing.
Or, when he returns
and she burns and longs,
she draws a serpent
meaning "that's you!"[28]   (44)

'What is the essence of life?' Madhav asked once again.
'Who is the love-god's spouse? Which is the chief of
flowers? And what does a girl do when she gets married?'

'Breath,' she responded in sequence. 'Rati, that is,
pleasure. Jati, which is the jasmine. As for the girl, when
she gets married she goes to the house of her father-in-
law!'[29]

Madhav said:

'There was a young and pretty girl
sporting in a jewelled bower,
she struck her husband with her foot
though he had done no wrong.'   (45)

Kámakandalá countered:

'Reflected was her image there,
she saw it and at once concluded
that he was with another wife,
so she struck her husband with her foot
though he had done no wrong.'   (46)

Madhav asked:

'The daughter of the mountain king,
clasped within her husband's arms,
just then saw Ganga on his head;
she is extremely proud, but why
and where did she begin to kiss him?'[30]   (47)

'She was so angry, she wanted to die,' replied
Kámakandalá. 'So she kissed him on the throat, on the
left, where the poison stays.'
    Madhav said:

'She trembles with desire
and longs to be embraced,
yet Lakshmi says, "No!"
and, "Look! Look! My lord!"
to Hari. Why so?'   (48)

'When Hari was looking at her she saw her own brother,
the moon, in his eyes, and felt abashed outside,'
Kámakandalá commented. 'It was an error, but that is the
reason.'[31]
    Madhav spoke again. 'It is the season of spring,' he
said. 'A diffident maid thinks that the god of love has
himself arrived with his bow bent in a circle and proceeds
to worship him with fragrant flowers in both her hands.'
    'The whirling line of bees is the god's bowstring,'
Kámakandalá observed, 'and if it breaks, love will fail.
That is what she has in mind.'[32]

'It is the season of summer,' Madhav continued.
'A girl is thirsty, and she goes to the river Ganga and takes
some of its water, bright as nectar, in her cupped hands.
She looks at it, but does not drink. Why?'

'Her hands are like tender new leaves,' Kámakandalá
responded, 'and the water glows with their colour. She is
afraid it may be blood.'

'It is night,' said Madhav, 'and a man tells his girl:

> "Do not stand outside, my darling!
> Come in quickly! It is the time
> when the eclipse demon comes.
> Seeing your face, which has no blemish,
> he may spurn the moon's full orb
> and swallow you instead!"[33]   (49)

He also recited the sequel:

> 'The maiden's face, a moon, beholding,
> and the pearl stars round her throat,
> the wild goose thinks it's night again:
> it's sunrise, but the poor bird weeps.'[34]   (50)

And continued:

> 'The infant Krishna, eating butter,
> shook his head, a fly to brush off,
> and the three worlds trembled too.'   (51)

But Kámakandalá spoke up in between. 'All the three

worlds are within Krishna,' she said, 'so even they are
bound to tremble when he shakes his head.'

Madhav posed yet another riddle:

> 'The chariot travels on the hill,
> the driver stays upon the ground,
> swift as the wind it goes around
> but moves not forward still.'   (52)

'That is the potter's wheel,' replied Kámakandalá.

Again he asked:

> 'In the woods there is a hero,
> he has no flesh or blood,
> but he cuts off heads, as of a foe,
> and keeps staying in the wood.'   (53)

'This is the cord for severing pots and other items of clay
which are on the potter's wheel,' Kámakandalá answered.

'O Kama!' cried Madhav. 'You are brilliant. You are
learned. At present there is no woman on earth to
compare with you.'

'O brahmin!' said Kámakandalá, 'you are the god of
love incarnate! There is no one in the whole world like
you. This has been the most happy night, but what will
happen in the morning? May the sun not rise at all! For,
what Shiva could not give to the tale of the triple city, nor
Hanuman to the Rámáyana, or Bhima to the Bhárata, that
grace my beloved has given to me!'[35]

'Don't get upset, my moon!' Madhav told her. 'The joy of your company fills my heart! The soul within is nourished by your grace!'

Thus did they spend the entire night, entertaining each other with riddles, rejoinders and such like. In the morning Mádhavánala, fearful of the king, began once again to prepare for his departure. It has been said:

> For family's sake
> give up one man,
> and for the village,
> the very clan,
> for the republic,
> the village forsake,
> but the earth entire
> for your own sake.[36]   (54)

The Parting

As he was about to leave, Mádhavánala spoke to Kámakandalá with great tenderness. 'You must remember me, my beauty,' he said, 'even though I have to go away.'

'For that, my lord, you must tell me how to remember you in rebirth.'

'Darling! Where is the question of such remembrances in this very life?'

'My life, traveller, goes with you. For me, this birth will be over today itself.'

At last Madhav sought Kama's permission. 'Let me go my love,' he entreated her. 'It's not possible for me to stay any longer.' These sad words hit her like a thunderbolt. 'To break out of my embrace and leave is no great feat,' she replied lightly. 'It would be something if you could quit my heart.' Then, bursting into tears, she flung her arms around his neck. He too could not maintain his composure, and wept as he left the lamenting girl.

Once he was out of sight, Kámakandalá collapsed on the ground, burning in the flames of separation. As goes the ballad:

> Dawn of youth and first love,
> separation in spring time,
> and exile in the rains,
> who can bear such flames? (55)

> Having to accept charity,
> living in another's house
> with a worthless spouse,
> then acting like a guest:
> O who can bear such fires? (56)

> In infancy, the loss of mother,
> in prime of youth, the loss of wife,
> in old age the death of one's child:
> all three are heavy sorrows. (57)

Regaining consciousness for a moment, Kámakandalá still beheld Madhav before her, and cried:

> 'The day becomes a thousand years,
> the night becomes an aeon,
> the moon's afire, sandal burns,
> food's like poison, and desire

is one's daily enemy too:
what is not torture for a girl
separated from her lover?'   (58)

Madhav listened and replied. 'The moon becomes
fierce like the sun,' he said, 'soft breezes turn dagger-
sharp. Garlands prick one like needles and clothes feel
like made of stone. Light turns dark. Life becomes a
burden. Alas, the time of separation is like the end of the
world.'

Kámakandalá listened and wept. 'Will you come
now, my love, or later, or when the day is done?' she
recited. 'Thus does a girl wait day after day for her
beloved, tears trickling from her eyes.'

'Don't delude me with cool and smooth leaves of
plantain, my friend. Don't you know that the wind makes
fire blaze even more?' replied Madhav.

'You have gone away, my love, after robbing me of
my senses and setting my heart on fire. To grace another's
home? But you will not be saved, my dear, even if you go
to the sacred Ganga,' lamented Kama.

'Happy the land where you have gone to embellish
someone else's house, traveller. Here all is desolate. How
will I see you again?

'Sandalwood and camphor essence,
a cooling flow of every fragrance,
recreation and mind's elation,
what will you obtain, my lord,
by going to someone else?'   (59)

'O my young beauty!' cried Mádhavánala. 'O you of the
radiant face and the graceful gait, of lovely eyes and
pleasing talk. How indeed will I see you again?'

'Now it is time for you to leave,' sighed Kámakandalá.
'For whatever reason you go, my charmer, may all your
hopes be fulfilled. If you chance to see a flower, give it my
name. Forgive me for what I may have said. I have no merit
at all, but remember me at least for my faults.

'May you meet with every success, my lord, but may
my tongue shatter into bits before I ask you to go. May my
shortcomings depart instead. May evil and affliction fly
away, but never good and worthy men like you.

'Go, if you must, my love, but don't look at the hands
with which I steady myself. It will be an unlucky omen if
what you have shaken so, were to fall down.

'Go, my love, if you must,
who can stop your going?
But your departure will be my death,
who can change what is fated?   (60)

'The vine of my spirit
has climbed to the bower
of your deeds and greatness.
Do not let it wither,
but nourish and nurture it
with the water of love.   (61)

'It is not for me to weep, for that will bring bad luck in the
attainment of what you want. If my eyes water, it is only

because they are troubled by the smoke from the fire of separation.'

'It is because of that very fire,' said Madhav, 'that, when asked by this sweetheart, the words "I am going" get stuck inside the lover's throat before they can come out. For on them depends the life of both.'

'If you are going after all, lover,' Kámakandalá responded, 'then go! May you have a happy journey. And may I be reborn wherever it takes you. For,

> 'In your absence, every moment
> will become an hour for me,
> each hour lengthens to a day,
> each day be no less than a month.'   (62)

For a while they argued thus with each other. Finally, Mádhavánala departed once again, his heart pierced by the sorrow of parting from Kámakandalá. It is said that some things lessen sorrow. These are: the mother's presence, the birth of a child, living with someone dear, expectation of wealth and a mistress late at night. But, living in exile during the rainy season, having little or no money in youth, and separation in the course of first love: these three are heavy burdens to bear.

Love in Separation

After Mádhavánala had gone, Kámakandalá once more fell to the ground, lamenting:

> 'Do me just one favour,
> O my heart, and break!
> How much sorrow will you bear?
> And, without the man I love,
> what will you do with life?   (63)

> 'O heart, you are like adamant,
> or are you made of diamond,
> that you did not shatter into bits
> when my lover went away?   (64)

> 'O God, do not create,

nor let mankind be born;
if born, don't let them love,
if in love, do not separate them; (65)

'O fountain of cooling water,
if your head were cut off too,
you would know the agony
of a simple person left behind. (66)

'You only think "why did I not take
my love with me?" as you depart
for other lands with my stolen heart.
I, a girl, these words repeat,
bereft by parting, all too weak:
the clouds at least will hear me speak.' (67)

On hearing her lamentations Kámakandalá's friends came
and consoled her. They took her inside the house where
she assumed the garb of an ascetic and began to spend her
days in fasting, sleeping on the ground and other celibate
practices. She gave up coloured garments as well as the
sixteen bodily ornamentations[37] and discontinued the use
of vermilion on her forehead, collyrium in her eyes and
the betel leaf in her mouth. She refrained from rich food
till Madhav's return, emaciated her body and lived
virtually like a widow.

It is said that this worthless body has one great merit:
it can bear the burden of whatever condition it is placed
in. As for nemesis, it will find a fault in every excellence:
the expanse of the ocean is full of undrinkable water; there

are blemishes in the moon and thorns on the lotus stem; one finds poverty in learning and parsimony in wealth; there is bad luck in beauty and separation in love.

Meanwhile Madhav wandered from village to village and forest to forest. Distraught with love, he would call out for his beloved and ask the birds about her. 'Tell me, you creatures,' he would cry, 'where is that gazelle-eyed girl, as beautiful as Rambha?' Standing before the koel and listening to its song, he would think of his sweetheart and fall down in a swoon. Like a gravely wounded soldier, an arrow-stricken deer or a fish pulled out of water, he had not even a moment's comfort. 'O Kama! O my darling! Look how I suffer in separation from you!' he would lament in the wilderness. 'Where have you gone, fair one? Let me see you at least today.'[38]

Troubled by hunger and thirst, Madhav saw a fresh-water lake where he quickly drank his fill and sat down beneath a mango tree to recover from fatigue. 'Kámakandalá will be at her home, remembering me,' he said to himself as he thought of her and lamented,

> 'How can I not think of her,
> in whose voice were these five tones:
> the flute, the vina, the lavali metre,
> the turtle dove and the koel's song? (68)

> 'The half-shut eyes, the trembling lashes,
> the bitten lip, the faint "no, no",
> the face I saw at passion's end:
> who can ever forget it?' (69)

At that moment, in the lake, he observed a pair of swans before him. The male had just kissed the female's mouth and was obviously wanting to mate with her. Seeing them, Madhav too was overcome with desire, and cried out to the bird:

> 'O swan, impart to my beloved
> something of your own feelings:
> the gift will be most apposite
> for love is valued everywhere.'   (70)

Vikramaditya

ᡦᢆᡕᢣᢞᢇᢇᢒᢦ

*M*adhav continued on his way. Proceeding along a road, he encountered a brahmin dispatched by King Vikramaditya to King Kama Sena with a conundrum.

'O traveller!' he called out, 'what is there in your hand?' 'It is a letter with a conundrum.' 'Show it to me.' The brahmin handed over the missive, on which was inscribed a single line

> The sea is floating on the ship.

Madhav saw that it was an unfinished verse, and completed the stanza which he wrote out:

> It was the pitcher-born sage divine,
> his cupped bands looking like a boat:
> seeing what was held inside them,

to the women there it seemed
the sea is floating on the ship.[39]   (71)

After solving the conundrum, Madhav travelled further
and came in due course to Ujjayini, the capital of
Vikramaditya. This king was a righteous ruler given to
helping others. He was famous as a hero of unequalled
valour, capable of dispelling the sorrows and soothing the
pains of others. Above all, he was devoted to dharma. It
is said that under the rule of such a monarch, the people
partake of pleasures at proper times and are always happy.
They are generous, brave and respectful of sacred rituals.
There is no fear of epidemics, enemies and external
threats. Money is available in millions. The rains come
when needed, the cows have full udders, the trees are
always covered with fruit and the earth with crops.

Such was Ujjayini that Madhav saw. At some places
there were gardens with trees in full bloom, at others step-
wells, lakes and incomparable temples. The women were
beautiful. The city looked like Indra's paradise but, so
smitten was he with love for Kama, that even there he had
no peace of mind.[40]

Madhav went to the city centre and asked for food at
some brahmin's house as he was extremely hungry. It is
said:

> It spoils beauty, makes one thin,
> destroys all thought of luxury,
> weakens thought, wears out restraint,
> and uproots dharma utterly.

It separates one from son and spouse,
it prunes the plant of modesty,
such is hunger, mother of sins,
which torments me so terribly.   (72)

The brahmin fed Madhav with all the devotion due to a
guest. It is said that no matter if he is a thief or a parricide,
an outcaste or a brahmin killer, one who arrives at the end
of the daily prayers is a guest bestowed by the heaven.
And, at the house from which he is turned away
disappointed, he takes away merit and leaves behind the
fruit of his own misdeeds.

Epistles of Love

*ftter the meal, Madhav sent a letter to Kámakandalá.
'I have reached Ujjayini safely,' he wrote. 'Please do
me the favour of writing how you are, and letting me know
quickly, so that my mind may rest.

> 'You do not know how exile
> has hid your lotus face from me:
> this skeleton wanders in the void,
> it lives wherever you may be. (73)

> 'As sages always God remember,
> and swans the holy Manas lake,
> as elephants wild the Reva river,
> and deer on rain clouds meditate.
> So I think of you each day,

longing your dear face to see.
It will be a blessed moment
when we will both together be. (74)

'As in summer, thirsty peacocks
think of clouds which will bring rain,
and lost geese of their scattered flocks,
so I long to see you once again.[41] (75)

'Where is the moon, and where the lily,
where the sun and the lotus flower,
the peacocks and the monsoon clouds,
the line of bees and the jasmine bower,
or the Mansarovar lake
where distant swans would like to stay?
Whatever one may cherish most,
one's karma keeps it far away. (76)

'Without you I have no sleep or solace at night,' Madhav
wrote further. 'All food appears unwholesome. Without
you, O lotus eyes, poison seems to course through me.
There was a time when I would not put a garland round
my neck for concern that it may separate us. And now
mountains, rivers, and forests lie between us!

'But being apart can never cause the loss of affection
between good and meritorious people,' he concluded.
'The moon may be far away and also covered by clouds,
but that does not lessen the lilies' love for it.'

Kámakandalá read Madhav's letter with deep sighs,
and sent him her reply:

'Thoughts of you are hidden in my bosom,' she wrote. 'I have strung a rosary of your virtues, and my days pass in telling the beads of our times together. I keep you in my heart. My ears are content in hearing about your merits, and my tongue in repeating your name, but my body writhes in agony for you.

'As the cow thinks of her calf, the wild goose[42] of the sun and the chaste wife of her lord, so do I long for you. As the chátaka bird[43] looks at the sky for raindrops when the monsoon arrives, so do I look for you. As the bee locked within the lotus by moonbeams longs for the sun, so do I long for you.

'Do not think, my darling, that love is lessened by distance. Among good people it becomes twice as strong. My body, sustained by thought of you like the lotus by water, is here, but my soul is wherever you are. For when one lives in another's heart, he can never be far, despite the distance. It is not like the eyes which cannot see the ears even though they are only away from them.

'As the chákora bird for the moon, the wild goose for the sun and the peacock for the rains, so do I count the days for your return. What can I say more with mere words? We two are in love like a pair of lovebirds.'

The Temple of Mahákála

❧

Mádhavánala read the letter sent by Kámakandalá and sighed deeply. He then went into the city and, wandering here and there, saw the temple of Shiva, known in Ujjayini as Mahákála.[44] Entering its hall, he recited a hymn in praise of the great god:

'Salutation to Rudra,
All Enduring, Soul Supreme,
Shiva, Shánta, Shambhu,
Ishán, Shárva, Shrikantha,
Vámadeva, Vrishánka,
Bhima, Bhayadáyi,
Mahadeva, Shankara,
the Endless, the Hidden,
the Blue-Throated, Lord of Parvati. (77)

'Morning and evening,
at the end of his prayers,
the person who chants
with folded hands
those nineteen names,
is freed of all sin,
praised by heaven,
and goes to Shiva
at the end of his life.'   (78)

After reciting the hymn and paying obeisance to Shiva
Mahákála, Mádhavánala lay down in the temple to sleep.
But alas, he could not, for sleep comes easily only to a
person free of sorrow, in whom happy thoughts repose,
and never to one whose mind, body and speech are
pining for someone else. Comfort and ease last only till a
person falls in love; once that happens the soul is delivered
to the beloved. Not to see the loved one causes anxiety; to
see her results in deep emotion. If she is offended, it is
wounding; if she goes away, it is distressing. There is
indeed no happiness when one is in love.

Two or three days passed this way. Eventually, one
midnight Madhav took a piece of chalk and wrote out two
verses on the temple wall:

The sorrows in one's heart
well up to the throat,
but once again subside;
there isn't a single person
in whom one may confide.   (79)

Rare are they who will
grieve in another's grief,
and cherish one afflicted;
ready to help another,
those who understand.   (80)

Then he fell asleep.

On the following day King Vikramaditya came to the temple at dawn to pray to Shiva. Noticing and reading the two verses which had not been on the wall earlier, he said to himself: 'The writer of these is in my city. He seems oppressed by the pangs of some separation and extremely dejected. This obviously goes against the principles of my rule, but I must first find out who this person is before I can dispel his sorrow.' Thinking thus, the king returned to his abode.

It has been written that clouds thunder in the autumn, but do not rain; yet in the monsoons they pour incessantly without much tumult. Similarly, the base prattle but do not deliver; the good, on the other hand, also act and not just speak. Deep minds are quiet, like deep waters; but they lead to action, unlike the shallow ones who make much noise and do nothing else. That night Madhav wrote another stanza on the wall:

Rama is no more on earth,
who apart from him will know
the sorrow of a lover's loss?
What can I do? Where can I go?[45]   (81)

The king read this verse when he came to the temple the next morning. He thought about it and declared: 'I will not eat till I have learnt what has made this person unhappy.' Having made this vow, Vikramaditya went home.

Now, it was the king's vaunt that:

My kingdom perish, and my person,
and so too may my sovereignty,
but the word which I have given
must stay on for eternity.   (82)

So he had a proclamation made by drumbeat in the city: 'Is there anyone here oppressed by the sorrow of separation? Whoever informs me of such a person will be given the reward he desires.'

While the drum was being beaten, the harlot Goga Vilasini accosted the drummer who explained the entire matter to her. 'O drummer,' she said, 'go to His Majesty and say that the king may dine in peace. I will carry out this task.'

Thereafter, Goga Vilasini roamed around the city. At the temple of Mahákála she marvelled to see a Brahmin laughing and weeping. He looked thin and frail and had a lute in his hands. Sometimes he would sing and sometimes keep silent.

In the evening, the harlot hid herself in the temple. Sometime after midnight Mádhavánala, who was sleeping among a group of ascetics, began to sigh deeply. Noticing this, Goga Vilasini approached him quietly and lay down

by his side, placing one leg across his body. At this
Madhav mumbled in his sleep: 'O Kámakandalá your
foot is on my body. Take it off, please.' Then he wept
aloud, crying, 'O Kama! Where have you gone? Why
don't you even look at me?'[46] Having listened to these
words and understood what the matter was, the harlot got
up from his side and departed.

The next morning she went to the king. 'Your
Majesty,' she said, 'I, your servant, have discovered that it
is a brahmin named Mádhavánala. He lives in the temple
of Mahákála and is exceedingly miserable on account of
his separation from Kámakandalá.'

The king was astonished. 'How did you learn all this,
Goga Vilasini?' he asked. 'Listen O King,' she replied,
'what goes on inside the mind can be discerned from the
appearance and the gestures, from behaviour and
movements and from the changing expressions of the face
and the eyes.'

Madhav meets the King

~

*R*ealizing that what Goga Vilasini had said was true, the king gave her the money she desired. At his orders some officers then went to Mádhavánala on the following day and brought the brahmin before the monarch. Madhav proffered the king a benediction and took a seat:

> 'May Kali, who is present
> in the murmers of the multitude,
> brave slayer of the buffalo demon
> and of Shumbha and Nishumbha,
> protect you, Lord of Men.'[47]   (83)

The king joined his hands in greeting. 'Brahmin, tell me what can I do for you,' he said. 'From where have you come, sir, and where is your permanent abode? What is your name and why are you so distraught?'

'My name is Mádhavánala,' Madhav replied. 'I was born in Pushpávati. I learnt all the shastras and earned respect in scholarly gatherings. But Govinda Chandra banished me, presuming I was of bad character and unreliable. So I went to Kámávati, seeking the patronage of some other lord.

'Kama Sena is the king there. He is well respected by both men as well as the gods. And in the city lives Kámakandalá who is the most alluring goddess of beauty.

'I fell in love with Kama. It has made me helpless and no food or anything else appeals to me now. But my love grows stronger by the day, like the moon waxing in the bright half of the month.'[48]

King Vikramaditya spoke kindly to Mádhavánala. 'Don't fall in love like this with a harlot, young man,' he said. 'Don't you know the way of such women? They are like the karaveer[49] flower. All its petals are crimson – the colour of love – but never its centre. The harlot's heart is also like that, no matter the devotion she may manifest. These women are full of wile and totally devoid of fine feelings and affection. Without money, even the god of love himself means nothing to them.'

'The harlot is like a cemetery,' the king continued. 'One man she consumes, like she would a corpse; the second, she guards in a coffin; and yet another she covets in the mind. Her house is a den of immorality. Even to go there leads to notoriety and brings the family into disrepute, apart from depleting the purse: it is therefore quite inappropriate for sensible people. You should know, Madhav, that for men to have intercourse with whores is like thrusting one's hand into a serpent's mouth, or making a diet out of poison.'

'There are great differences between individuals,' Madhav responded. 'This applies to men and women just as much it does to horses and elephants, metals and woods, stones, waters and textiles. All women are not the same, Your Majesty. Search all the three worlds, but you will find no one to compare with Kámakandalá. Just as every mountain does not bear a mine of rubies, nor every forest the sandalwood tree, she too is someone as rare.[50] As for me, the swan can only live at a lake of fresh water, where bees hum over lotuses awakened by the sun.'

The king, however, continued with his admonition. 'These ladies of the street,' he said, 'put love aside and please one only with what will eventually prove disagreeable. The lover may never know it, but once he has been won over, they renege on their commitment. Who indeed is dear to such women? They chatter with one, make eyes at another, yet think all the time of a third. Intelligent people know that what goes into their hearts is no more than so much silt into the river and water into the sea.

'Lies and daring,' he added, 'are a part of women's nature, as are delusion and folly, uncleanliness, cruelty and an excess of greed. They are veritable witches: to look at them is to lose one's senses, to touch them one's strength and to sleep with them one's vital force. The wise can understand the movements of the sun and the moon, the stars and the planets, but never the goings-on of women. Their nature is the same as that of water and base people: all three keep away from eminence and overwhelm that which lies below.'

Madhav listened with attention to the king's words. 'Your Majesty,' he said, 'Kámakandalá may be a harlot, but I love her very much. There is no joy, no delight in the world greater than the happiness a woman gives. It brings together all that causes fulfilment. No pleasure can compare with it, just as no chariot can with one drawn by horses, and no draught with one of milk.

'Of flavours, the essence is ghee,
and of ghee, the ritual oblation,
of that the essence is but heaven,
and heaven's quintessence is woman.   (84)

'Who made woman
a lake of nectar,
a trove of pleasure,
a mass of joy?   (85)

'Of all the jewels upon this earth,
than woman none is finer;
for her alone one looks for wealth –
it has no use without her.   (86)

'She is a vine with fivefold fruit:
progeny, pleasure, solicitude,
prestige without the family
and to paradise the key.   (87)

'Affluence is dharma's fruit,
and comfort that of prosperity,
but women are at comfort's root,
without them it's a nullity. (88)

'One who never did embrace
a lovely girl with lotus face,
tender limbs, and dulcet speech
with words well joined each to each,
the feel of flowers on her skin
soft as moonlight streaming in,
citron breasts and cherry lips,
pretty teeth and graceful hips:
his birth, his life, his prosperity,
meaningless must always be. (89)

'Is it love, when you no more curse the moon?' Madhav
added, 'nor listen to the sweet messages brought by the go-
between? When your body does not waste nor your breath
choke with sighs? When your darling is at your disposal
and you embrace yet still neglect her? This happens only
in the married state which you labour to observe.

'The nectar taste of woman's lips
and limbs the man who never knew,
on earth what did this animal
ever really know or do? (90)

'For, of all the sites of pilgrimage
woman is the best and true,

the man who went there not, on earth
whatever did this animal do?'   (91)

'It's only those with minds obtuse
who, in things of no clear use,
abstractions, whose consequence
for pain or pleasure makes no sense,
see salvation from the worldly round.
For me, the wanton, moaning sound
of a girl, wild-eyed with passion,
as she turns in eager fashion
and then her knotted skirt unties:
that is where salvation lies.   (92)

'For if one does not lie with a girl glowing like a lotus
flower, or use the sword in battle to gratify one's lord, nor
rescue kinsmen mired in poverty, what is the point of
being born and troubling one's mother?

'It is only due to past good deeds that one finds a lotus-
woman, whose eyes twinkle and girdle bells tinkle. Her
breasts are hard, her navel deep and her hair braid like a
coiled serpent.[51] With ruby-red lips and tender limbs radiant
like the new moon, she is truly delectable. Moreover, she is
always ardent and longing for union and accomplished in
all the sports of love. She deserves to be enjoyed with a glad
heart; otherwise one should recourse to the river Ganga,
with its white banks and scores of holy sages.

'Make your home by Ganga's waters
which may all your sins remove,

or by the garland on the bosom
of a charming girl you love.'   (93)

King Vikramaditya marvelled greatly at Mádhavánala's
words. 'O Madhav,' he said, 'in this city there are many
women like Kámakandalá. Take the one who pleases
you. Besides, if you need some money or any such thing,
I will give you all that. But give up this craving for
Kámakandala.'

Madhav did not agree. 'This young bee has drunk at
will of the nectar from screwpine blossoms,' he said. 'It
has spent moonlit autumnal nights within the lily's
sanctum and flitted about the rut-stained temples of
elephants. How can it bind itself to some thorny bush of
kareer?'[52]

'O Mádhavánala!' the king exclaimed. 'The bees
which have flourished on elephant's ichor, and perfumed
their bodies with the pollen of lotus blooms, are
sometimes fated to pass time on bushes of lime, sunflower
and kareer!'

But once again Mádhavánala replied as he had done
earlier. 'O King!' he said, 'even though there may be
lotus-filled waters everywhere, the wild goose's heart is
never at ease without the Mansarovar – the lake of the
heart. Moreover, this earth may still quake, though held
up[53] by the cosmic elephants, the divine tortoise and the
sacred serpent king: but the dedication of a pure-hearted
man will remain firm, even till the end of time.'

It is said that at this juncture Madhav also made a
request to the monarch. 'Listen, Lord Vikrama,' he said,

'you are known as the Dispeller of Others' Sorrows. This is the time to prove it. I will quote to you but one line of a verse which is found in scores of sacred books. It is that "merit lies in helping others and sin, conversely, in persecuting them". What is gained, it may be argued, by the birth of someone who cannot fend for himself? Equally, what is gained in the birth of someone who is able but unwilling to help others? I ask you, therefore, to bear witness to these sayings and reunite me with Kámakandalá.'[54]

The king pondered. 'Madhav has no interest in other women,' he said to himself. 'One respects only that of which one knows the qualities. The grapevine may flourish, but the crow prefers the bitter nimba[55] fruit. The heart will not accept, without proof, mere beauty and attractiveness as love, just as camphor will not neutralize borax without gold. So, in some way or the other, I must bring Kámakandalá to Madhav. For this I will need to go to Kámávati with him.'

The King's Decision

～⚬～

His mind made up, King Vikramaditya quickly summoned his generals. 'Whatever army I have,' he commanded, 'cavalry and elephants, chariots and infantry, young, old, and juvenile, let them all set forth.'[56]

Blazing with splendour like a second sun, King Vikrama then marched out towards Kámávati with Mádhavánala and a fourfold army. The earth quaked at its march. The dust raised by the horses' hooves filled the sky and covered the sun, turning day into night. The ensuing darkness distressed even ghosts, spirits and similar creatures with foreboding that the end of the world was at hand. Blessed indeed is King Vikrama who set out thus, leaving behind his city, progeny and kingdom, to dispel the sorrow of a stranger.[57]

In a short time they neared Kámávati. When they

were ten miles from that capital, Vikrama halted his army.[58] 'I must find out if Kandalá's love is as great as that of Madhav,' he said to himself and, leaving his troops behind, he went alone to the city. Intent on putting Kámakandalá to a test, he proceeded to her house.

'This is no ordinary man,' Kama said to herself, as she saw the king arrive. Mindful of this and thinking of Mádhavánala in her heart she entertained the ruler in various ways. As she knelt before him, he placed his foot upon her breast in token of a proposition, but she dismissed it in that very moment, pushing the foot away with her hand.

'You fool!' said the enraged king. 'Why have you refused my foot? Don't you know who I am?'

'I know that you are some king,' she replied. 'But listen to my explanation. In my heart dwells a brahmin named Mádhavánala. That is why I rejected the foot you placed there.

'The sacred fire is honoured as the guru by all the initiates,' she continued, 'the brahmin by all the castes and a guest by all the people; but for women the husband alone is the honoured guru. Further, gods and gurus are not to be touched by the foot nor spoken about with vulgar familiarity, for it is like slaying them without a weapon. Anyone who does that is bound to go to hell.'

King Vikramaditya was taken aback at the unusual reply. 'Tell me, girl,' he asked her gently. 'What is it that afflicts you? Why do my words of love give no comfort to your heart?'

'Nothing afflicts me,' she replied, 'except the separation from Madhav. My heart is so full of love for him that it has no room for your words.'

'This girl seems as much in love with Madhav as he is with her,' said the king to himself. 'I shall make every effort to bring them back together. But there is still one more test which I must put her to.'[59]

'O Kámakandalá,' he then said, 'there was a brahmin named Mádhavánala in Ujjayini, who died recently. He was weeping at that time for a sweetheart from whom he was separated.

> 'It was spring, a vernal breeze
> blew, fragrant from the flowering trees,
> filled with the humming sound of bees.
>
> Of his girl some traveller thought,
> with longing was his heart so wrought,
> it broke – he died upon the spot.'[60]　　　　(94)

Kámakandalá was deeply affected on hearing of Mádhavánala's death from the king's own lips. 'O beloved!' she cried, and collapsed in a faint. Within moments life had left her body.

It is said:

> Hoping does not let you die
> when death alone will bring true love,
> not to die at such a moment
> for love will an embarrassment prove.　　　　(95)

When the heart has burst
like a bubble lacking water,
know that, in mankind, to be
true love in all its verity.   (96)

The king was amazed. Filled with apprehension and sorrow he returned immediately to his camp and told Madhav all that had transpired with Kámakandalá.

'O Kámakandalá! You are no more?' cried Madhav as he heard the news. And he too fell down unconscious and breathed his last, like a fish removed from water.

The king was plunged in grief. 'Alas, my words were ill chosen,' he lamented. 'I behaved like a fool and am now guilty of murdering a brahmin as well as a woman. It is said truly:

'Rash, unthinking action,
always in disaster ends.
Fate looks for those who act with thought
and to them success sends.   (97)

'With such a calamity having occurred, my vast empire is now worthless. How can I atone for what I have done?'

Cursing himself thus, he picked up the royal scimitar to cut off his head with his own hands. But at that moment he was restrained by the vetála, the familiar spirit, who had just arrived. 'Why, O King, are you set upon such a desperate act?' he asked, taking the sword away from the monarch's hand. 'Your grief-stricken subjects will perish in your absence. Truth itself will lose all meaning without a king like you. Therefore, your life deserves to be safeguarded. Why give it up for no purpose?[61] Choose a boon, for I am pleased with your intrepidity.'

The king recounted all that had happened. 'If you are pleased,' he told the vetála, 'then bring this woman and this man back to life.'

The vetála proceeded to the nether world and returned within moments with the nectar of immortality. 'Take this, Your Majesty,' he said, 'and make Madhav drink it.' That done, the brahmin arose, crying, 'O Kama! O my dearest! Where are you? Why don't you speak?' The king was utterly delighted.

His mind at rest, the wise Vikrama then put on the garb of a physician and went quickly to the house of Kámakandalá. Her companions were weeping as they tried to revive her. Doctors kept coming and going. 'I am a physician,' the king called out loudly at the door.

A companion took him to Kama. 'She is dearer to me than life, doctor,' she said with folded hands. 'If she were to breathe again, I will give you my own life, not to speak of much money.' The king gravely poured the nectar into Kámakandalá's mouth, whereupon she too arose and, remembering Madhav, began to weep.

The king was like a sea of compassion. Having consoled Kama he mounted his horse and hurriedly returned to his own camp. There, seated upon his throne, he consulted his wise counsellors. 'You are experts in statecraft,' he said, 'tell me what should be done in this situation.'

After much deliberation, the ministers came to their best decision. 'The use of force is not suitable here,' they concluded, 'nor is there need of financial inducement. There should be no occasion for any of these if the objective can be attained by negotiation and conciliation. This is the way confident powers proceed.

'So, some competent envoy should be deputed. He should be a person of good family, as well as astute. One without lineage or character will for certain ruin any chance of success.'[62]

Diplomacy and War

~~~~~~

*K*ing Vikramaditya then surrounded Kámávati with his army and dispatched an emissary to Kama Sena. The envoy was Shripati. Full of enthusiasm and concern for his duty, he proceeded immediately to the lord of Kámávati.

'I am the emissary of Vikramaditya, sent to your king,' Shripati told the gatekeeper, who went inside and informed his master. The wise king then directed four experienced attendants to bring the envoy in and, after welcoming him, spoke to him with due ceremony.

'Who are you, sir, and for what purpose have you come?'

'I am the ambassador of Vikramaditya. My name is Shripati. King Vikramaditya lives for the welfare of others. There is no untimely death in his land. All the people are at peace. None is in distress. There is only one, named

Mádhavánala, who is suffering because of separation from his beloved.'

'This lover in distress arrived by chance in Ujjayini,' Shripati continued. 'It is for his sake that our king is at your frontier with an army. In Your Majesty's city lives Kámakandalá, for whom Madhav pines. Kama too is devoted to him. Hand her over to my master.'

Kama Sena took the envoy's words as an insult. 'What are you saying, you fool!' he cried, biting his lip angrily. 'Don't you understand my power that you use such language in this royal assembly? It will besmirch my honour if I were to give Kandalá away. Other kings would belittle me for having surrendered my property out of fear. For a proud warrior, death is better than such denigration. Go, tell your king there can be no question of giving up Kandalá.'

Shripati turned conciliatory at these words. 'King Vikramaditya has no intention of war,' he said. 'He has no other request but that Your Majesty give Kandalá to him. If you, my lord, desire war, let me say this to you in all frankness. Our king is given to helping others. He grieves at seeing their grief. He comes to you as a guest deserving of hospitality. Show him that and be at peace.'

'I am aware that Vikramaditya is as you say,' the king replied. 'But I cannot tolerate ignominy. Your king should remember the warrior's code and give up hope for Kandalá. And if it is a question of arms, give me a challenge to go to war.'[63]

'O Monarch,' the emissary then said to Kámávati's ruler, 'listen to the final words of Vikramaditya: "You must send Kámakandalá to me immediately. No delay will be tolerated. Or else, my army and I will destroy you and your city and take her away by force."'

'What should I do?' Kama Sena wondered on hearing this message. 'There is no king on earth to equal Vikramaditya and he has addressed me in such language! But Mádhavánala is also with him. Therefore, I cannot possibly surrender Kámakandalá.'

'Ambassador,' the ruler then replied, 'go to Vikramaditya and tell him that Kama Sena says the following: "How is it that you have brought Mádhavánala to my land, when I had expelled him? It is for this reason that I will not surrender Kámakandalá."'

The emissary returned to Vikrama's camp and reported what he had been told. The king was incensed. 'Go back, ambassador,' he commanded, 'and tell Kama Sena that if he has the strength, let him come out and fight the battle.'

The emissary went back to Kama Sena and told him all, whereupon that king readied himself for war. Vikramaditya also moved forward with his army. Nearing the city, he sent his envoy once more.

'O Kama Sena,' said the ambassador. 'Listen to what Vikrama says:

> 'The frog may croak most angrily
> before the lord of beasts himself,
> but the lion won't give way to rage
> at such a creature: what's the point?'   (98)

This verse infuriated Kama Sena even more. 'I will not hand over Kámakandalá without a battle!' he thundered. On receiving this reply through the emissary, Vikramaditya said sternly: 'Today I will destroy Kama Sena and his army.'

The Lovers Reunited

❧

Thereafter Vikrama's soldiers entered Kámávati and Kama Sena also came out with his troops. A fierce battle raged for one full day, in which the army of Kámávati was defeated. Its infantry and cavalry, its chariots and elephants, were struck down by the attacking forces and the Kámávati army was completely routed.

'What should I do?' Kama Sena worried. 'It was foolish not to surrender Kámakandalá earlier instead of acting contrarily. Now Vikramaditya has annihilated my army for the sake of Madhav and the girl.'

Having pondered over the matter, Kama Sena took Kámakandalá to Vikramaditya and fell at his feet in submission. 'Pardon! Pardon!' he cried, surrendering the courtesan, 'I am your slave. Grant me safe conduct.'

'You fool! Why didn't you hand her over to begin with?' said the victorious king. 'You have lost your forces for nothing. Yet, what could you do? What had to be has happened and no one must be blamed for it.'

Vikramaditya then summoned Madhav and said: 'O Mádhavánala, accept Kámakandalá and give up your grief.' With these words he gave her away to the young man, who was overwhelmed with joy, as was the girl.

The king then made peace with Kama Sena and, restoring him to his throne, returned with Mádhavánala and Kámakandalá to Ujjayini. There he gave much wealth to Madhav who enjoyed all the pleasures of life with his beloved.

> Lanka had to be won,
> the sea crossed on foot;
> the enemy was Ravana,
> the help, only monkeys.
> Yet Rama alone
> defeated the demons.
> The success of great men
> depends on their prowess,
> not on assistants
> or clever expedients. (99)

The two lovers lived together happily for a long time and, when it was up, they both went to heaven. For,

> The rising sun is red as blood,
> so too is the pomegranate bloom:
> when two lovers their blood unite,
> it is a treasure priceless. (100)

Epilogue

~~~

One must always merit gather
by appropriate means whatever:
thus will a person happy be,
have long life, luck, prosperity.   (101)

The person who this story hears,
which the name of Madhav bears,
will not suffer grief or pain
of separation in love, ever again.   (102)

The Afterstory

〜❦〜

Pleasant is a paste of sandal
and even more the moonlit night;
but, to be with one's beloved,
is of all the best delight.   (103)

*H*is pledge redeemed, King Vikramaditya returned to
his country along with Madhav and Kámakandalá.
They were welcomed back in Ujjayini where the king
entrusted Madhav with many duties.

Madhav worked for the king and earned a hundred
thousand dinars each day. He was also granted five
hundred prime villages with lands and temples. Reunited
after a long time, the lovers revelled day and night in each
other's company. They would bless King Vikramaditya
repeatedly for affording them such happiness. 'You are
rightly called the Dispeller of Others' Sorrows,' they

would say, 'there is no one like you in all the three worlds.'

One day Madhav, worrying that he had not seen his parents for long, sought the king's permission to visit his ancestral home. This was accorded and Madhav was also provided with a vast sum of money, a trove of rubies, pearls and others gems, four thousand horsemen, sixty four elephants and many foot soldiers.

Setting out with this retinue, Madhav arrived in due course at the city of Pushpávati. King Govinda Chandra trembled with fear, even as he tried to ascertain whose forces had approached his capital. 'From where has this army come?' the people wondered. 'Are they friends or are they foes? And who is their leader?' Deeply worried, they gathered with the chief of the citizens to consider what should be done to avoid battle with what seemed a numberless horde.

The chief of the citizens was the highly respected priest Shankara Dása. 'Do whatever is needed to protect my realm,' the king told him. 'I give you authority to act so as to prevent a war.'

Madhav had no idea what lay ahead as he approached the city's centre. When Shankara Dása arrived the younger man immediately recognized his father and fell at his feet. 'The unbelievable has happened!' he thought to himself, as the priest also acknowledged his son and embraced him, his old eyes streaming with tears. It was a moment of great joy for both father and son. Seeing them together, the king and the people were greatly reassured.

The meeting turned into a most festive occasion. People were delighted and the city decorated, as everyone greeted Madhav. Kámakandalá met his mother and paid her respect. She also met his brothers and sisters and their families. Everyone was overjoyed.

For Madhav, it was happiness beyond measure to be with his parents and family. He stayed amidst them with Kámakandalá, enjoying all comfort and prosperity. The king gave him high honours and he lived like a god. In course of time four sons were born to him and his wife.

All this pleasure and enjoyment, says the poet Kushala Lábha, was a testimony to the results of meritorious action. It is no surprise that those who come from a good family and follow the rules of righteousness should attain this end. But Kámakandalá was born to a harlot. She was endowed with youth, wealth and vivacity: yet she kept her sheel, that is character and conduct, pure and immaculate.

Men and women who maintain their character and conduct spotless and pure will enjoy happiness in this as well as the next world. It is sheel which makes humankind godlike and bestows all joy. To conduct oneself like Kámakandalá did will give all that one wants. She lived the rest of her life at ease and did many pious and charitable works before she passed away, returning to a welcome by all the gods in paradise.[1]

Endnotes

～～～

Introduction

1.   Balbir Singh (ed.), Máhavánala-Kámakandalá-Charita, (Uttar
        Chand Kapur & Sons, Delhi) publication date not indicated,
        but the editor's introduction is dated 27 September 1953. The
        information on manuscripts and retellings in this section is
        derived from the introduction and appendices to this work,
        hereafter referred to as Balbir Singh. However, a single page
        ms, fragment at the Asiatic Society, Kolkata, (No. 10240) is
        wrongly dated as Samvat 1788 in that study. The actual date in
        this Nagari script text, as physically seen by the present
        translator, is Samvat 1188. This, if taken as the Vikrama era,
        would correspond to AD 1130, thus predating the story's textual
        evidence by about 300 years.

2.   Balbir Singh. Tale 91 of Triyacharitra in Dasam Granth.

3.   Maurice Winternitz, History of Indian Literature, Vol. III,
        Subhadra Jha (tr.), (Motilal Banarsidass, Delhi), 1985.

4.   C.M. Ridding (tr.), Kádambari (of Bána), London, 1896; Tales of the Ten Princes (Dasa Kumára Charitam) by Dandin, A.N.D. Haksar (tr.), (Penguin Books India, New Delhi), 1995.
5.   Chandra Rajan (tr.), Vetála Panchavimshatiká of Sivadasa, (Penguin Books India, New Delhi), 1995; A.N.D. Haksar (tr.), Simhásana Dvátrimshiká, (Penguin Books India, New Delhi), 1998.
6.   None of these appear to have been translated into English. The last mentioned was in a translation into German by A. Weber, 1877.
7.   Balbir Singh.
8.   For example, in the well-known histories of Sanskrit literature, respectively by M. Winternitz and A.B. Keith.
9.   M. Krishnamachariar, History of Classical Sanskrit Literature, (Motilal Banarsidass, Delhi), 1976 (Reprint).
10. As detailed by Majumdar in his introduction to Mádhavánala-Kámakandalá-Prabandha, cited in our Introduction and hereafter referred to as Majumdar.
11. Balbir Singh. Apart from giving extracts from the gazetteer, he also describes photographs of the Kámakandalá ruins.
12. Pia Guerrinha (ed. and tr.), Mádhavánala-Kathá, Pisa, 1908.
13. Balbir Singh.
14. While Majumdar gives no further information about this ms., from the details of the title and the opening verse reproduced in Balbir Singh it would seem to be the same as no. 157 in Aufrecht's Catalogue of Mss. in the Bodleian Library, Oxford University. It should be added that Majumdar mentions that a second volume of his book would have more details about ms. and other subjects, but this is not listed in available records and may not have been published.

The Story

1.   The goddess of speech and learning in the Hindu pantheon. Often invoked at the beginning of a literary enterprise, she is

usually described as radiating a snow-white aura, holding a vina or lute in her hands and seated upon a white swan. The second stanza of the Prologue is the opening verse of Mádhavánala-Kámakandalá-Carita ascribed to Jodh Kavi and hereafter referred to as Jodh.

2.   Identified with momordica monadelpha, a plant hearing bright red fruit to which women's lips are often compared to in Sanskrit literature.

3.   This accords with the categorization given in Kámasutra of Vatsyayana and other ancient Indian texts on erotics. The physical and other attributes of the different types of women vary in some works, but are broadly similar.

4.   All three are well-known figures in Indian mythology. The god of love, known by many names the commonest of which is Kama, is visualized as a young man of extraordinary beauty armed with a bow and five-flower arrows. One of his names is Makaradhvaja or one bearing a banner with the image of a crocodile or mythical fish. Shukra and Brihaspati were divine sages who were the preceptors, respectively, of the demonic and the godly beings.

5.   This and the three preceding paragraphs are taken from Jodh vv. 10-20.

6.   Raga is a basic element of Indian classical music. Its dictionary meaning is 'a pattern of notes used as a basis for improvisation' or further elaboration. Also described as a melodic entity, the raga has numerous forms. A popular method of classifying them is in terms of ragas (masculine) and their wives, called raginis, usually personified and associated with particular scenes or moods. The number of ragas is commonly given as five or six, each having six wives.

    This rendition and the three preceding sentences are based on vv. 143-146 and 148 of Mádhavánala Kámakandalá Chaupai by Kushala Lábha, hereafter referred to as Lábha. The

– 86 –

following verse, which is from the Baroda text, but also included in Lábha, praises music as of equal importance as the four well-known Vedas.

7.   This and the two preceding paragraphs are based on Lábha v. 151 and vv. 14-23 of Mádhavánala Kathá of Damodara, hereafter referred to as Damodara.

8.   Ravana, abducted Sita in the well-known epic Rámáyana. Bali was a mythological king who lost all his dominions by the magnanimous but imprudent pledge of a gift to an incarnation of the god Vishnu.

9.   This and the preceding sentence from vv. 27-29 of Jodh.

10. Rati is the wife of Kama, also see note 4 above. The word also connotes pleasure as well as sexual union.

11. Identified with sesamum indicum. The nose is often compared to its flower as a sign of beauty in Sanskrit literature.

12. The mythical mountain of gold. This sentence is from Jodh v. 34.

13. This and the preceding sentence is from v. 44, Jodh.

14. The reference is to three incarnations of Vishnu: as Vámana, who received the gift from Bali, see note 8 above; as Rama, who forded the sea on way to Lanka to rescue his wife Sita; and as Krishna, who lifted Mount Govardhana to shelter the cattle and the herders of Gokula during a rainstorm.

15. The details of the offering are from Jodh; the Baroda text has only a fivefold offering.

16. Based on Damodara, v. 274.

17. The celebrated author of Nátya Sástra, the principal treatise on dance and drama.

18. From Jodh, vv. 53-56.

19. From Damodara, v. 282.

20. Using song and music to catch wild animals was a hunting technique reported, among others, by the eleventh century scholar and traveller Abu Raihan al-Biruni in his account of

India, chapter XVII, Alberuni's India, E.C. Sachau (tr.), Ainslie Embree (ed.), New York, 1971. For Bali see note 8 above. Karna, another exemplar of magnanimity, is a prominent figure in the well-known epic Mahábhárata.

21. Brahma, Vishnu (also called Hari) and Shiva (also called Shambhu) are the gods, respectively, of creation, preservation and destruction in the Hindu pantheon. The term 'celestial singers' here refers to gandharvas, a class of semi-divine beings who were also the musicians of the heavenly world. Madálasá was the learned and pious daughter of a gandharva chief. She was abducted by a demon and taken to the nether world of the dead, from where the music of her kinsmen rescued her. Sarasvati is the name, both of a goddess as in note 1 above, and of a sacred river which flows down from Mount Kailasa, the abode of Shiva.

22. This bird was supposed to drink water only in the form of falling raindrops.

23. Three epic kings who suffered exile and other misfortunes with great fortitude.

24. This and the two preceding sentences are based on Damodara, vv. 330, 346 and 358.

25. A sage regarded in tradition as the father of Sanskrit prosody.

26. The sixty-four arts or kalás are enumerated, among other texts, in Saiva Tantra a the list which can be seen in Sanskrit, but without any translation, in M. Monier Williams' Sanskrit-English Dictionary, New Delhi, 1988 (reprint). A wide-ranging inventory, it has been grouped here under six convenient sub-headings by the present translator who has also consulted the list given in Adarsha Hindi Shabdakosha, Varanasi, 1976. (1) Nine performing arts: singing dancing, playing musical instruments in general, playing the lute and the timbrel, playing water-based instruments, conjuring, sleight of hand, dramatics and costuming. (2) Twelve fine arts and crafts: drawing,

painting, decoration with powdered rice and other grains, making garlands, bed making, repair work, vastu, masonry, making floral spreads, crafting floral carts, cane weaving, and image making. (3) Four household skills: cooking, making alcoholic and other drinks, needle work, and spinning. (4) Eight arts of maquillage: applying beauty spots, tinting limbs and garments, cleaning hair, braiding hair, perfuming, make-up, jewellery and skin care. (5) Thirteen skills of learning: gem appraisal, metal appraisal, minerology, gemology, arboriculture, knowledge of languages, sign language, knowledge of good and bad omens, poetry, extempore versification, lexical knowledge, prosody. (6) Twelve games: setting and solving riddles, capping verses, reading aloud from books, completing verses, slanging, cock and quail fights, water games, gambling, wrestling, hiding clothes, children's games, and games of seduction. The nature of the six other kalás in this formidable list appears obscure.

27. The tale of Jayanti and Madhav is taken from Lábha, vv. 14-23, 57-71, 77-81, 100-114; the education of Kámakandalá from Lábha, vv. 114-119; and Madhav's recollection from Lábha, vv. 193-204.

28. In the original this stanza constitutes a play on the double meaning of the Sanskrit word bhujangah, which denotes a serpent as well as a lover.

29. The answer is an indirect comment on the allusion to sexual intercourse contained in the question. See note 10 above.

30. The verse refers to Goddess Parvati, daughter of Himalaya, king of the mountains. Here, she is depicted as jealous of the river goddess Ganga whom her husband, the god Shiva, held upon his head when she flowed down from heaven to earth. Shiva also bears inside his throat a poison which, in another myth, he had swallowed to save the world. This is alluded to in the sentence following this verse.

31. Hari is one of the many names of the god Vishnu. His wife, goddess Lakshmi, was born from the ocean at the same time as the moon, which makes the latter her sibling. In another myth, the moon and the sun are the eyes of Vishnu in his cosmic form.

32. See note 4 above. The string of Kama's bow is visualized as being formed of a line of hovering bees. They, and the flowers which attract them, are associated with the season of spring, who is a close companion of Kama.

33. The conceit in this verse is based on the tradition that eclipses occurred when the demon planet Rahu swallowed the full moon or the sun. The face of the beloved is often compared to the moon, but it may be even more desirable to the demon as it is also free of any blemish.

34. The bird was supposed to feed on the pollen of lotus flowers, and eagerly to await daybreak when they opened.

35. The reference is to heroic characters in Shiva Purana, the Rámáyana and the Mahábhárata. For some the comparison may seem inappropriate as Shiva is a more exalted figure than the other two.

36. This well-known verse also occurs in other works, for example the Mahábhárata, as also Chanakyaniti, Hitopadesa and Suka Saptati.

37. In tradition these sixteen items of maquillage are: body rubs, baths, dresses, coiffure, application of kohl in the eyes and vermilion in the hair parting, decorating soles of the feet with colour, auspicious marking on the forehead, beauty spots, use of henna and of perfume, polishing and tinting the teeth, chewing betel, reddening the lips and wearing a garland.

38. This paragraph from Jodh, vv. 88-91.

39. This verse is an example of the literary pastime, samasyá vinoda, mentioned in the Introduction. A provocative statement is contained in its last line, and explained by

improvising the first four which also complete the verse. This is done by drawing on the legend of Agastya, a divine sage born from a pitcher into which the seed of a god had fallen. This sage, who is known by several appellations, drank it up. Hands cupped together to hold some liquid, or a single hand contracted for the same purpose, can look like a little boat – hence the conceit in the completed verse.

40. This paragraph is from Jodh, vv. 74-77.

41. Here taken from Jodh, v. 159, the verse is also included in Damodara Sanskrit, v. 608.

42. See note 34 above.

43. See note 22 above.

44. The temple of Mahákála stands in the present day city of Ujjain in Madhya Pradesh.

45. This is a double reference to the divine hero, Rama. Like the writer of the verse, he too suffered separation from his beloved wife. He was also an ideal king who cared and felt for his people, as is expected of Vikramaditya.

46. This sentence is from Jodh, vv. 115-116.

47. Kali is one of the names of the great goddess who, as Durga, slew the demons mentioned in the verse.

48. This and the three preceding paragraphs are from Jodh, vv. 121-126.

49. Identified with oleander (nerium odorum), the root of which is supposed to be poisonous.

50. This and the preceding sentence are from Lábha, vv. 518-519.

51. From Damodara, vv. 690-692.

52. Identified with cappris aphylla, a thorny plant growing in deserts.

53. According to Puranic mythology.

54. This paragraph is from Lábha, vv. 527-530.

55. The lime tree fruit.

56. From Jodh, vv. 142-143.

57. From Jodh, vv. 145-147.
58. This and the next sentence are from Jodh, vv. 148-149.
59. This and the two preceding paragraphs are from Jodh, vv. 156-160.
60. This is a Sanskrit stanza from Lábha, v. 573.
61. This and the two preceding sentences are from Jodh, vv. 181-182.
62. This and the five preceding paragraphs are from Jodh, vv. 185-189, 190-194, 206-210.
63. This and the six preceding paragraphs are from Jodh, vv. 213-229.

The Afterstory

1. The entire section is from Jodh, vv. 623-654.

List of Verse Renditions and Sources

〜

*G*iven below are serial numbers of the verse renditions in this translation. With each is also given the original stanza number from the Baroda or Ananda text. The stanzas taken from the supplementary texts of Jodh, Lábha and Damodara are sourced as such!

Details of the texts are included in the Introduction.

1.	1	29.	54	57.	116	84.	203
2.	Jodh, v.1	30.	55	58.	117	85.	204
3.	6	31.	63	59.	123	86.	205
4.	11	32.	71	60.	131	86.	205
5.	13	33.	72	61.	132	87.	206
6.	14	34.	80	62.	135	88.	207
7.	15	35.	81	63.	138	89.	208-210
8.	16	36.	82	64.	139	90.	212
9.	17	37.	83	65.	140	91.	213

10. 18	38. 84	66. 141	92. 214
11. 19	39. 85	67. 142	93. 217
12. 20	40. 90	68. 145	94. Lábha Sansk. v573
13. 21	41. 91	69. 146	95. 226
14. 22	42. 92	70. 147	96. 227
15. 23	43. 94	71. 148	97. 228
16. 26	44. 95-97	72. 153	98. 229
17. 27	45. 99	73. 156	99. 230
18. 28	46. 100	74. 157	100. 231
19. 35	47. 101	75. Jodh,v.159	101. 232
20. 40	48. 102	and Damodara	102. 233
21. 41	49. 105	76. 158	103. Lábha,
22. 42	50. 106	77. 172-174	Sanskrit v.623
23. 43	51. 107	78. 175-176	
24. 44	52. 108	79. 180	
25. 50	53. 109	80. 181	
26. 51	54. 112	81. 184	
27. 52	55. 114	82. 185	
28. 53	56. 115	83. 187	

About the Author

Aditya Narayan Dhairyasheel Haksar was born in Gwalior and educated at the Doon School and the universities of Allahabad and Oxford. A well-known translator of Sanskrit classics, he has also had a distinguished career as a diplomat, serving as Indian High Commissioner to Kenya and the Seychelles, Minister to the United States, and Ambassador to Portugal and Yugoslavia.

His translations from the Sanskrit include the Hitopadesa and Simhásana Dvátrimshiká, both published as Penguin classics, and the Jatakamala published by HarperCollins India with a foreword by H.H. the Dalai Lama. He has also compiled a Treasury of Sanskrit Poetry, which was commi-ssioned by the Indian Council for Cultural Relations.